NETTIE AND NELLIE CROOK

ORPHAN TRAIN SISTERS

NETTIE AND NELLIE CROOK

BASED ON A TRUE STORY

NETTIE AND NELLIE CROOK

ORPHAN TRAIN SISTERS

BY SUSAN HILL WRITING AS

✦ E. F. ABBOTT ✦

WITH ILLUSTRATIONS BY CLINT HANSEN

FEIWEL AND FRIENDS NEW YORK

A FEIWEL AND FRIENDS BOOK
An Imprint of Macmillan

NETTIE AND NELLIE CROOK: ORPHAN TRAIN SISTERS. Text copyright © 2016
by Macmillan. Illustrations copyright © 2016 by Clint Hansen. All rights reserved.
Printed in the United States of America by R. R. Donnelley & Sons Company,
Harrisonburg, Virginia. For information, address Feiwel and Friends,
175 Fifth Avenue, New York, N.Y. 10010.

Our books may be purchased in bulk for promotional, educational, or business use.
Please contact your local bookseller or the Macmillan Corporate and Premium
Sales Department at (800) 221-7945 ext. 5442 or by e-mail at
MacmillanSpecialMarkets@macmillan.com.

Library of Congress Cataloging-in-Publication Data

Abbott, E. F., author.
Nettie and Nellie Crook : orphan train sisters / E. F. Abbott. — First edition.
pages cm. — (Based on a true story)
Summary: Twin sisters Nettie and Nellie Crook are taken away from their dysfunctional
parents in 1910 when they are only five years old, and placed in an orphanage—
at six they are put on the orphan train by the Children's Aid Society and moved
from New York City to Kansas, ending up in a household where they are
treated more as servants than children.
ISBN 978-1-250-06835-4 (hardcover) — ISBN 978-1-250-08033-2 (e-book)
1. Children's Aid Society (New York, N.Y.)—Juvenile fiction.   2. Orphan trains—
Juvenile fiction.   3. Orphans—New York (State)—New York—Juvenile fiction.
4. Twins—Juvenile fiction.   5. Sisters—Juvenile fiction.   6. Child abuse—Juvenile
fiction.   7. New York (N.Y.)—History—Juvenile fiction.   8. Kansas—History—Juvenile
fiction.   [1. Children's Aid Society (New York, N.Y.)—Fiction.   2. Orphan trains—
Fiction.   3. Orphans—Fiction.   4. Twins—Fiction.   5. Sisters—Fiction.
6. Child abuse—Fiction.   7. New York (N.Y.)—History—1898–1951—
Fiction.   8. Kansas—History—20th century—Fiction.]   I. Title.
PZ7.1.A16Ne 2016   813.6—dc23   [Fic]   2015004154

Book design by Anna Booth & April Ward
Feiwel and Friends logo designed by Filomena Tuosto
First Edition—2016

1   3   5   7   9   10   8   6   4   2

mackids.com

*To the Orphan Train Riders
and their families*

BASED ON A TRUE STORY BOOKS

are exciting historical fiction about real children who lived through extraordinary times in American history.

———◦◦◦———

DON'T MISS:

John Lincoln Clem: Civil War Drummer Boy

Mary Jemison: Native American Captive

Sybil Ludington: Revolutionary War Rider

NETTIE AND NELLIE CROOK

ORPHAN TRAIN SISTERS

CHAPTER 1

Nettie Crook sat at the kitchen table and swung her dangling feet in time with her sister Nellie's. The girls were five years old, identical twins. They loved to trick people into mistaking one for the other. Father could be fooled, but never Mama.

It was wonderful to have a sister as a best friend. Even when Father was gone for weeks at a time—Mama, sometimes, too—Nellie was always there. But one twin is always a little bit older than the other, and it bothered Nettie that her sister was the one born first. Nettie's birthday was even celebrated a whole day *after* Nellie's each year. Nellie was born late in the night of January 23, 1905, and Nettie was born in the small hours of the next morning, January 24. It didn't seem fair for one twin to be a whole day behind the other one in life. Nettie made up for being second any way she could.

Nettie picked up her doll from the table and set her in her lap. "My Min's prettier."

"Dolly's just as pretty," said Nellie.

"Says you." Nettie crossed her eyes at Nellie. *Dolly* had to be the worst name ever given to a doll.

The dolls had been birthday presents this year. Mama had made each one from a wooden spoon on which she'd painted black curls, a red smile, and china-blue eyes with dark lashes. It was the first and last birthday they would celebrate in this apartment.

"Why do we have to move again, Mama?" Nettie said.

"Father's through at his job." Mama leaned over a cardboard box to place a newspaper-wrapped dish inside, straightened up, and pushed a lock of hair from her face. "We have to move so that he can find some other work."

"Leon works," Nettie said. Their brother, Leon, was not at home. He was almost nine years old—old enough to help Mr. Mead at the butcher shop sometimes after school. Mr. Mead would give him a few pennies to wash the floors and scrub the walls with a bucket and rags.

"Not that kind of work, not a coin tossed our way now and again. A family needs steady money to live in a house and put supper on the table."

Nettie swung her dangling feet thoughtfully. She'd heard Father talking about dredging the Erie Canal the last time he was home, some weeks ago. He'd sat around the table with his friends, drinking from bottles that clinked. The low laughter and gentle murmur of the men was a comforting sound in the night as the girls fell asleep in the bed they shared. "Where will we go?" Nettie asked.

"When will we go?" said Nellie.

Mama glanced at Sissy, the twins' younger sister, napping in a cradle pushed up against the wall. She offered a tired smile. "Come here, girls." She pulled out a chair and sat in it, leaning heavily against the back, and patted her lap. "Come here to me."

Nellie and Nettie scrambled out of their chairs and

climbed onto Mama's lap, one on each knee. Like Father, Mama was often gone, sometimes for long stretches of time, and the girls and Leon didn't know why. They didn't know that she was a very young mother, and awfully tired and unhappy. They didn't understand that their little sister was sick, and that Father's work wasn't steady. But they knew they loved their mama, especially when she took them on her lap and told them a story.

"Once upon a time," Mama began, "there were two little twin princesses, as fair as fairies, as gentle as lambs, and as strong and true as an oxen team."

This sounded so silly that the girls always laughed. "Baaaahhhh," went Nellie, and "Mooooo," went Nettie.

"And the twin princesses loved each other very much," said Mama, "and always cared for each other, no matter what. Isn't that right, girls?"

Nettie nodded solemnly. They surely did. Especially if the twin who was older by a whole day was apt to cry and needed the younger twin to stand up for her.

A sound came from the cradle. Mama scooted the girls from her lap, cutting the story short. "I just bet this next place will be our forever home," she said.

Forever home. Maybe. But they had heard those words before. Mama had said "forever home" when they moved the last time, and the time before that.

⟞⟩◦◦◦⟨⟝

At first, Nettie liked their new apartment. Though it was dark and gloomy, she liked the playful way Mama's kerosene hurricane lamp cast flickering shadows on the walls at night. She pretended the shadows were birds or fairies from Mama's stories, come to life. It was cozy, sleeping in the same room with Mama and the baby

The exterior of a tenement in New York City, sometime between 1900 and 1910. *[LC-DIG-det-4a20846]*

A family living inside a New York tenement house in 1911.
[LC-USZ62-91915]

and Leon. Nights that Father was home, his snoring kept Nettie awake, and even that she liked because it meant he was there.

But time went on, and Father didn't come home very much. The baby got sicker and sicker. The little apartment seemed darker. The shadows leapt and darted like sharp-toothed demons.

And then came the day the shadows seemed to swallow them up. Nettie and Nellie's little sister died. There were candles at the head and foot of the small coffin at the church. Mama stood by the coffin and stared at her hands. She didn't speak. She didn't put her arms around her children to comfort them. Nettie stood close to Nellie, shoulders touching, and squeezed her hand in a pattern, *one-two-three*. I-love-you. Nellie squeezed back.

Not many people came to the church, but kindly Mr. DiSopo, the grocer, was there. He took off his canvas cap and pressed it to his chest, praying softly in Italian words they didn't understand. His wife, Nettie knew, had been sick and died, like Sissy. His oldest daughter had gone away to work long hours in the Triangle Shirtwaist Factory. "Seven dollars a week," Nettie had heard Mr. DiSopo tell Father, "nine or more hours a day, plus Saturdays, sewing ladies' blouses." He stood there worrying his cap and crying.

"Everything is upside down," Nettie whispered to Nellie. "Mr. DiSopo's crying, and Mama isn't."

⸺⸺⸺

The day after Sissy's funeral, Mama left home and didn't come back for weeks. Father was gone, too. The twins went out alone to ask Mr. DiSopo for bread, and he gave them loaves of coarse rye, some apples, and some eggs. Leon earned twenty-five cents selling newspapers.

Then Father came home. When he saw the dirty kitchen, and the children's filthy clothes and sooty faces, he yelled at them.

"What have you done? Where is your mother? Can't you even wash your own faces?"

"Who cares about our old smudgy faces?" Nettie made two fists and stomped her foot. "You better ask how we been feeding our own selves!"

Father's face reddened, and one hand shot up high as if he was about to hit Nettie.

Nettie stared him down. "We don't know where Mama is," she yelled over Nellie's crying, "any more'n we know where *you* are when you're gone!"

There was a silence and time froze—with Father's fist raised high, Nettie glaring fiercely at him, and Nellie holding back her sobs with both hands.

In the next moment, Father seemed to turn his anger on the kitchen table, where there wasn't any food. He slammed his fist down on it, hard. He slammed the door that Mama wasn't walking through. And when the latch didn't catch and the door creaked slowly open, he slammed it again as if to shut it up.

Nellie grabbed on tight to Nettie, jumping fearfully

with each blast of harsh noise. "Stop it! Somebody, help us!"

As if in answer to Nellie's cry, the door flew open. It was Mama. She and Father stared at each other a long moment. Slowly, he lowered his fist. He seemed to get a whole size smaller. Mama came inside. Father put his arms around her.

Maybe this time, Nettie thought, things would get better. At least they were all together again now. Maybe things would change.

CHAPTER 2

Mama's return did not make things better. But one day, change did come. It was early on a morning in December of 1910. Father was gone again. The sky was overcast, and snow tumbled lightly outside the apartment. The world seemed muffled and sounds came soft—Mama's soapy hands rubbing wet cloth against the washboard, Leon shoveling coal into the stove, a man's heavy footsteps coming up the outside stairs, and then, at the door, a knock.

Mama opened the door. She stood there, hands dripping, as a man they didn't know removed his hat.

"Mrs. Crook," said the man, "may I come in?"

Nettie hugged herself and hunched her shoulders to her ears. The man spoke in a low, gentle voice, but still he was scary. He was big, his coat all shoulders and buttons, and he wasn't one of Father's friends come to call. He told Mama he was the justice of the peace.

Mama said nothing but stepped aside to let him pass. She lowered herself into a kitchen chair slowly, as if she'd suddenly become an old woman.

The man reached into his chest pocket and pulled out a sheaf of folded papers. He opened them on the table in front of Mama and spread them flat. "I've come to take the children," he said.

Mama sat very still. She didn't look at him. She didn't look at Nettie or Nellie. Leon was still standing by the stove, dumbly holding on to the coal scuttle as if he'd forgotten what such a thing was for.

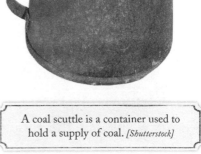

A coal scuttle is a container used to hold a supply of coal. *[Shutterstock]*

Nettie felt Nellie's hand in hers, and she squeezed it. "Mama?" Leon broke the silence.

Mama nodded once at Leon, and he set down the pail of coal and stepped to her. "Come here, girls," she said, "come here to me." Nettie and Nellie sat one on each knee, as they'd done many times before on good days when Mama was happy. She was not happy now.

"Mama. Once upon a time," Nettie prompted. Mama's hair was greasy. Nettie couldn't remember the last time any of them had bathed.

But Mama shook her head and drew her lips in. "Not this time, girls. No story this time."

Mama was crying. She hadn't even cried at Sissy's funeral. The man with the papers must have brought very bad news.

The justice of the peace had been told about the Crook children, the children whose father was often gone for weeks at a time, and whose mother could not be counted on to stay and care for her family. He'd seen many such children, and many worse off than these.

Nettie watched the man as he dragged a big hand down over his eyes, nose, and mouth, as if he wanted to wring out the thoughts he'd stored up behind his face. She wondered who had told on them. Was it Mr. DiSopo? But he had been so kind to them. He'd given them bread and apples and eggs. And hadn't she done a good job taking care of Nellie, just like twin princesses always did in stories?

Not ten minutes later, the man with the papers told the children to come with him. Mama sat at the table and did nothing to stop him. One by one, Leon, Nellie, and Nettie hugged Mama good-bye.

When it was Nettie's turn, she held on tight. "Say something, Mama!" Nettie said. She knew she was just this side of crying—her throat ached and her nose was filling up—so she buried her face in Mama's shoulder and breathed in the smell of her, pressing her cheek against the soft cotton of her blouse. "Don't you let him take us, Mama," Nettie whispered. "Please don't let him."

Mama stayed very still. Then she reached up and pried Nettie's arms from around her neck. Nettie swallowed back what felt like rocks in her throat. "Mama. Please, Mama." Mama's hands dropped to her lap. She did not raise her eyes to meet Nettie's.

Nettie turned away from Mama and followed Leon

and Nellie out the door and down the stairs. She looked
back once—was it Mama she heard? Was it Mama
crying? Her feet kept moving, without sensing the
ground. Her hand was numb to the man's big hand,
helping her up into the wagon. She sat but didn't feel
the seat beneath her. The wagon began to move. The
horse's hooves must be clopping, Nettie thought. The
man must be speaking, because his mouth was moving.
Leon was saying something back, and Nellie was crying, but all of it made no noise. All Nettie could hear
was that sound, that awful sound—muffled, ragged, as
if her throat was full of rocks, like Nettie's—the sound
of Mama crying.

Nettie sat in the wagon and kept her eyes on the horse's ears, so she wouldn't look back. She mustn't look back.

Nettie and Nellie were just five years old. They would never see Mama again.

CHAPTER 3

The wagon stopped before a big building with dark windows that stared out from under gable roofs. Towering trees stood sentry outside the front steps, their bare limbs like the bony arms of giants, waiting to grab and scratch and hold. It was the orphanage in Kingston, New York, and this is where the man with the papers left the twins and Leon that snowy day in December of 1910.

Nettie followed Leon up the steps to the great door. Her breath made little clouds, and she squeezed Nellie's hand, *one-two-three. One-two-three.* She could hear Leon breathing shallowly as the door swung open on heavy hinges.

"Step inside, hurry up." It was a gray-haired woman dressed severely in black, with black heeled boots that buttoned up the sides of her ankles. The set of her mouth was as grim as her clothing. "Welcome to Kingston. I am the matron," she said in a voice that offered no welcome at all. "Don't let in the cold."

But the orphanage *was* cold. Standing inside, Nettie shook with it, and Nellie's hand was like ice in hers.

"This is where children come to live when their parents are—"

An orphans' home from the late nineteenth century. *[LC-USZ62-53535]*

"Our parents are not dead," Nettie interrupted. She knew what an orphanage was. "Don't you say that."

The matron fixed Nettie with a flat stare. "Dead or not fit to care for their own, it's all the same. Their children—you children—are burdens to society," the matron said. "You will live here from now on."

"No!" Nettie said, and swallowed hard. Were Nellie and Leon just going to stand there staring at their shoes? Had they given up already?

"Children with such beginnings are seldom adopted," said the matron. "Especially not twins, I should think. Especially not one who doesn't know her place," she scolded, pointing right at Nettie. "Now, say good-bye to your brother, girls."

Nettie had to scowl, or else she might cry. They'd already had to say good-bye to Mama. "Why do we have to? Where's he going?" she demanded to know.

"Boys and girls are housed separately here," said the matron.

Nettie felt sorrier for Leon than for herself as she watched him walk away and disappear into a different section of this terrible, cold place. Nettie and Nellie, at least, would have each other. Wouldn't they?

The matron led the girls to the dormitory, a room lined with small cots. She gave them each a set of new clothes—a new jumper and top, underthings, a nightgown, and a new pair of boots that buttoned up the sides like hers. Nettie picked the clothing off her cot. She reckoned she couldn't even count as high as the number of beds in the great, long room.

Soon it was mealtime, and it was a good thing, because the girls hadn't eaten anything since their sliced-bread-and-no-butter breakfast with Mama back at home. What was Mama eating for supper? Nettie

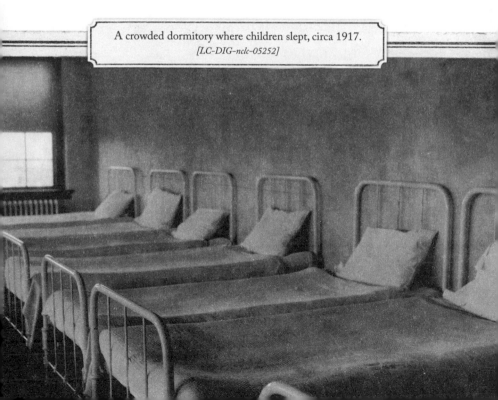

A crowded dormitory where children slept, circa 1917.
[LC-DIG-nclc-05252]

Young children eating their dinner at an orphans' home in Iowa, circa 1918. *[LC-USZ62-119508]*

wondered. Was she all alone? Would she come for them? Would Father?

They sat at a long table. Like birds at a feeder, other girls came and sat, and the room became noisy with chatter and movement.

"Quiet!" came a shout from the matron. The chattering stopped almost instantly.

Nellie and Nettie sat shoulder to shoulder. Someone set a shallow pie tin before each of them. In the pan was a ladleful of thin soup, with some bits of carrot and onion floating in it. Was Leon eating the same supper?

He was older and bigger. The pan of watery soup would hardly make a dent in his hunger. Nettie ate it all up, and still she was hungry.

The matron strode the length of each long table, arms crossed over her chest. When she walked by them, Nellie spoke. "Excuse me," she said, using her most polite voice.

Nettie elbowed Nellie in the ribs. "Keep quiet," she warned.

The matron stopped and put her hands on her hips. "What is it?"

Children under the care of the Children's Aid Society.
[LC-DIG-ggbain-01461]

Nellie held up her empty pie tin. "May I please have some more?"

Matron gave her answer with a swat that sent the pie tin clattering on the table. Everybody heard. Nellie tucked her chin to her chest and shut her eyes tight.

Matron took a stub of pencil and a little black-bound book from her apron pocket, ready to make a note. "Which one are you?" the matron demanded to know.

"Nellie," came the whispered reply.

Matron put pencil to page.

Nettie sat up straight. "She's fibbing. She's *Nettie*. *I'm* Nellie."

The pencil stopped. Matron looked at Nettie with pursed lips and knotted brow.

"No, I'm Nellie, like I said." Nellie shook her head, and tears plopped onto her cheeks. Now Matron looked from Nettie to Nellie, and a couple of girls giggled. Matron's face got red.

Matron narrowed her eyes at Nettie, and then again at Nellie, clearly confused about which girl was which. She closed the little book and put it in her pocket. "I've got my eye on you," said the matron. "I've got my eye on you both."

When the matron walked on, Nettie put her arm around her sister. "Don't cry," she whispered. "We can't cry here."

Although there was no talking allowed, some of the other orphans looked curiously at Nellie and Nettie. One girl with tangled red hair pointed at the twins' matching hair ribbons, and grinned. She pulled at her own red mop and crossed her eyes comically. They sat silently on the hard bench till everyone was finished.

In the dormitory that first night, Nellie and Nettie met some of the other girls and learned their stories. They were not the kind of stories Mama ever told.

"I was minding my own beeswax, asleep on a steam grate on the sidewalk, when they got me," the girl with the tangled red hair told them. Her name was Brenda O'Hare. "My mum died, my dad was long gone, and I took to the street. Where else could I go? What else could I do?" Brenda said. "I sold matches, is what. I was good at it, too."

"Not good enough," said a sturdy girl known as Bucky. "If you was really good, you might have made it on your own, and not be stuck here in this prison." Bucky glared at Nellie and Nettie. "Because that's what it's like, you know," she said. "Prison. Walking in straight lines, doing what you're told, and working, always working."

"Are you orphans?" Nellie asked them.

"Yeah. Just like you."

Nettie couldn't let that go. "We aren't orphans. We have a mother and a father, both," she said.

"Not according to the state of New York," Bucky said. "Your parents are as good as dead."

Brenda O'Hare nodded, her red tangles bobbing. "They'll even change your birthday on your records," she said. "They changed mine, anyway."

Bucky agreed. "So you can't be traced. They don't

want you having nothing to do with your family now."

"Don't look back," Brenda said. "That's what they tell you. Don't look back."

Nellie and Nettie changed into nightgowns provided by the matron and lay down on their small cots. A few minutes later, Nellie crawled into Nettie's bed with her.

"Tell me a story," Nellie whispered. Her tears dampened the pillowcase.

"Once upon a time, there were two little twin princesses," Nettie whispered, just the way Mama always began.

"And they were as fair as fairies, as gentle as lambs, and as strong and true as an oxen team," said Nellie.

"Right," said Nettie. She chewed her cheek, thinking a minute. "One day," she went on, "an evil wizard came and stole them from their nice kitchen and their own mother, and took them to a dark stone castle in the woods. They had to stay put, or else the evil witch whose castle it was would boil them in her terrible soup, and use their bones to pick her teeth."

Nellie sniffed. "This story isn't helping me to sleep."

"Well, listen," Nettie whispered, "later on in the

story, those twin princesses will figure out how to get away, so you can go ahead and dream about that."

"They don't sound as gentle as lambs," Nellie murmured.

"No," said Nettie. "They sure don't." She took Nellie's hand and squeezed it, *one-two-three*.

CHAPTER 4

"How did you end up here?" Nettie asked the other girls one day. They were on their hands and knees in the entryway, scrubbing with rags. The harsh soapy water stung the cracks in Nettie's fingers. Her sleeves hung below her wrists, and she paused to push them back above her elbows. The orphan children's clothing was passed around—patched and mended till it wore too thin.

"Street rats," said Brenda O'Hare, with a nod at Bucky. "That's what the police called us." She leaned back on her heels and pushed her bangs off her forehead with a damp wrist. Though it was cold in the orphanage, hard work made them sweat. "They trapped the street rats, and here we are." She took up the rag and scrubbed more vigorously at the wood floor.

"How are orphans made, let me count the ways," Brenda went on as she scrubbed. "Parents die of typhoid." *Scrub*. "Or fever." S*crub*. "Or flu." *Scrub*. "Parents come from Italy or Ireland, and don't speak English, and don't make enough dough to keep their kids in bread." *Scrub*. "They don't have gardens and chickens, like they did in the old country. They don't have enough to eat." *Scrub-scrub*.

"And don't forget the bottle," Bucky said. "My pap hit the bottle first thing in the morning, and by noon he'd be hitting me upside the head." She squeezed out her sodden rag. "I found a hole under a staircase I could live in, nice and cozy."

"Lots of us," Brenda agreed. "Too many of us. Too many mouths to feed. Cramped apartments and houses, and not any bit of room for one more."

"Specially not *two* more," Nettie said with a glance at Nellie. She leaned into her rag but stopped when she heard the heavy *ka-lump* and lighter *ka-lip* of approaching footsteps.

With Matron came a tall woman with fair hair that softly curled. She wore a green coat, a hat with a feather, and shoes with two-inch heels. It wasn't anybody Nettie remembered ever seeing before. The lady stopped and looked down at Nettie, and then at Nellie. She tilted her head and smiled.

"Hello," said the lady. She looked straight at Nettie when she said it. Her cheeks were brushed with pink, and her lips were painted red. Nettie thought of her spoon doll, Min.

"Hello," said Nettie.

The red lips parted, as if the lady might say something more, but the matron took her by the arm and hurried her away. Nettie stared after them. She was still staring when the lady looked back over her shoulder. "Come along, miss," said the matron, jerking the lady's arm so firmly that she stumbled. The feather in her hatband wobbled.

Nettie glanced at Nellie, a question in her eyes. *Who was that?* Nellie shrugged.

They were dumping the buckets of dirty water outside at the base of the big trees when the feather-hat lady came out the door and hurried down the steps, the matron close on her clippy heels.

"Matron's sure giving that lady the bum's rush," Nettie muttered to Nellie.

The lady stopped and looked at the girls, gloved fingers pressed to her red lips. "I'm sorry," she said. Then she turned away and climbed into the waiting buggy.

They stood and watched her go. Nettie and Nellie picked up their empty buckets and began walking toward the steps where Matron stood. "What's she sorry about? Who was she?" Nettie asked.

"Your aunt," said Matron.

The bucket handle slipped from Nellie's grasp. "We have an aunt?"

Nettie threw her bucket down and started running as fast as she could. Maybe she could catch the buggy on the road. She could try. Faster and faster she ran, out to where the drive met the road. "Wait!" she hollered. "Wait!"

But the buggy didn't stop. Soon it was gone from sight.

Nettie turned around and strode back to the orphanage, where Matron was still standing on the bottom step, arms crossed over her apron, and Nellie's bucket was on its side at her feet, as if something important had all spilled out.

"You better say she's coming back," Nettie said, glowering at Matron.

"Is she?" Nellie smiled eagerly.

The look on Matron's face told Nettie the answer before Matron even opened her mouth.

"She will not return," the matron said. "Better to sever all ties with the past."

This was too much. Nettie stomped her foot. "You old battle-ax! You didn't even let us talk to her!"

The matron puffed up and glowered at Nettie.

"Insolent girl!" Then she lowered her chin and seemed somehow to soften. "Have faith," she said. "It is better to start fresh than to go back."

⸺⸙⸺

If it had been one of Mama's stories, the mysterious aunt would have taken them from the orphanage. She'd live in a pretty yellow house with a kitchen table painted white, and boxes bursting with blooming flowers on the front porch steps. But it wasn't a story. Something their family had done must have been very bad, Nettie thought, to make the matron keep them in the orphanage instead of letting their aunt take them away with her.

Was it better to know, or not to know?

CHAPTER 5

After the visit from the mysterious aunt, the days stretched longer and felt more hopeless. Work began for the children at five in the morning. Often Nettie and Nellie tried to pass the time by talking about Mama and Father and Leon and Sissy, but that only made them feel worse. Every day seemed mostly the same, except for the variety of work: chopping wood, scrubbing floors, and laundering linens.

One day was different from the others. The orphans woke to a snow-covered wonderland. To their surprise, the matron told the children to put on their coats and go outside. Every limb and branch and twig of the tall trees in front of the building was softened and gentled by puffs of white. And parked on the packed snow at the foot of the orphanage steps was a royal-blue automobile, with a black top and white wheels. Seated inside was a pleasant-looking man in a big woolly coat. He had a big mustache to match his furry coat-collar, and kind eyes behind round spectacles.

"Pops!" Bucky squealed.

The man hopped out of the automobile. "Hairy drive, I can tell you," he boomed. "Had to have a horse team pull my Buick out of a snowbank! Tell Cook to heat up a pot of water, quick-quick!" he hollered to the matron, his mustache wiggling. "Got to fill my radiator with hot water, else it'll freeze and pop at the seams! And a blanket! A blanket! Must protect my beloved engine from the cold, just like my beloved children!"

The matron addressed the orphan girls. "If it was up to me, we wouldn't any of us be out here in the cold, not for a minute," she said, her hand on the doorknob. "You waifs can thank Mr. Everett Jansen Wendell for such frivolity."

Brenda O'Hare stuck two fingers in her mouth and let out a commanding whistle, the ends of her red hair poking out with enthusiasm below her bonnet. "Thanks, Pops!"

"You're most welcome, my darling ragamuffins!" he bellowed. "Everyone! I've brought sleds for you to play with. Let's not let all this good snow go to waste, shall we?" And with that, the big man tugged a couple of wooden toboggans from the back of the auto and put them on the snow. Then he crouched and began to pack snowballs in his gloved hands.

Tobogganing in New York in 1904. Toboggans are sleds that can be used for transport or recreation. *[LC-USZ62-34975]*

"Is he someone's father?" Nellie wondered aloud.

"Probably, but none of ours," Bucky said. "He's filthy rich, but I don't hold that against him. He acts regular, even though he gives buckets of money away, and lots to Mr. Brace's Children's Aid Society. Doesn't act like some fuddy-duddy who knows better than poor, pitiful us, know what I mean? He's only the best person around," she said.

Laughter filled the air, at least for a couple of hours on one winter's afternoon. They threw snowballs and made a tunnel to crawl through on hands and knees, and then they built a snowman so tall they couldn't reach to put the head on top. The girls were struggling to lift the last round ball when Pops took it from them and placed it squarely on the snowman's middle.

"A handsome specimen of a snowman as ever I've seen," Pops said. He clapped the snow off his gloves. "Will you introduce me to your fine cold-weather friend?" he said to the twins, a merry glint in his eye.

"This is Leon," Nettie said. The girls still hadn't seen their brother, and Nettie wondered if they'd ever see him again.

"Pleased to meet you, Leon," said Pops to the

snowman, and stuck out his hand.
"But you've no hand to shake.
Most ungentlemanly."

Nettie grabbed two twigs
from the snow beneath
the big old trees and
stuck them in the body
of the snowman.

"Fine, that's fine,"
said Pops, taking a
twig in his fingertips.
"And a fine day to you,
Master Leon Snowman."
He winked at Nellie and
Nettie. "Keep up the good work, my ladies. All will
be well."

Nettie wanted to believe Pops. But it was hard to
imagine that all would be well. They'd lost their little
sister, their father, and their mother, and now maybe
even their big brother, all in such a short time.

That night, Nellie climbed again into bed with
Nettie. Matron tried to stop Nellie from "wasting a
good bed" by not sleeping in it, but the twins could not

fall asleep unless they were close together, as they'd been from the time even before they were born.

"Nettie?" Nellie whispered.

"What?"

"Do you think this is going to be our forever home? An orphanage?"

Nettie stared up into the darkness. She couldn't see the ceiling, high above them, only the dark. She thought of Mama, and the many "forever homes" they'd lived in. Now they were alone, in an orphanage. It sure looked like this was it. Forever.

"Go to sleep," Nettie whispered. She clutched her spoon doll and lay awake a long time before she finally drifted off.

CHAPTER 6

Nellie and Nettie Crook lived at the orphanage for month upon month, while the world outside Kingston went on without them: 1910 became 1911, but they heard little of life beyond the tall trees out front. Their only knowledge came from snatches of conversation overheard between the matron and the cook or Mr. Fry, the old handyman.

"A nightmare," said the matron one day. "Dreadful news." She shook her head. "Dead. Every last one of them, dead."

Nettie saw her own fear in Nellie's eyes. *Who had died?*

Mr. Fry replaced his hat on his head, and when he

turned to go, Nettie followed him out the kitchen door. She caught up with him and tugged on the hem of his jacket.

"Please, Mr. Fry," she said, "who was it?"

Mr. Fry stopped. "Who was what?" he said.

Nettie swallowed hard. "Was it my mama and father who died? Tell me! Was it my brother, Leon?"

Mr. Fry rubbed a hand down his face. "No, Nettie, no. Poor lovie, it weren't your mum or dad we spoke of. There was a terrible fire at a factory. The Triangle Shirtwaist Factory. All the garment workers were locked in, so's they wouldn't take breaks or get out. So they'd stay and work—work their fingers to the bone. Most all of 'em girls and young ladies. So when the fire started up . . ." He sniffed and shook his head. "All that lint and them cloth cuttings. The fire roared to blazes, and the workers—they couldn't get out." Mr. Fry looked at Nettie. "Near a hundred-fifty, all dead, lovie. It's terrible sad."

"Did you know anybody who worked there?" Nettie asked.

Mr. Fry shook his head. "No," he said. "But many a man did. Many a man's daughter worked the shirtwaist factory, many a man's young wife." He removed his hat, ran his hand through his hair, then put his hat back on. "We can be thankful we've a roof over our heads this day, and loved ones by our side, eh?"

Later, Nettie burned her arm by accident on a steam pipe radiator. The cook treated the wound with raw egg, but the skin bubbled up, raw and blistered.

"Hurts like the dickens, does it?" Cook said, clucking. "That'll scar, that one."

Nettie cradled her burned, bandaged arm to her stomach and thought about the fire at the shirtwaist factory. She remembered the kindly grocer Mr. DiSopo, who cried beside Sissy's coffin. His daughter, Nettie knew, went to work at the shirtwaist factory. She hoped Mr. DiSopo's daughter had not been at the factory that terrible day.

Spring came, and at last the forsythia bloomed at the base of the great trees out in front of the orphanage, bringing a touch of yellow cheer. One morning in May, Nellie and Nettie were sent outside to beat the rugs, which the matron had hung out over a line behind the orphanage. Beating the rugs was a welcome chore. It was dirty and tiring, and the dust clouds choked, but it was good to be outside on a spring morning, and good to have a job the twins could do together.

"Let's pretend it's a jump-rope game," said Nellie. They took turns beating the rug, in time to a counting rhyme.

"Not last night but the night before
Twenty-four robbers came to my door—"

Something caught Nettie's eye. "Did you see someone?" She peered in the bushes alongside the road.

Then they heard a noise, like a kitten mewling.

They dropped the rug beaters and followed the noise. It came louder as they rounded the front of the building. They hurried up the steps. There, beside the door, was a basket. Inside the basket was a bundle of brown blanket and a little tiny face, all screwed up and crying.

"It isn't very loud, for a baby," Nellie said.

"Is it a boy or a

girl?" Nettie wondered. "I hope it's a baby girl, like Sissy."

Nellie smiled. "I wish she could be our little sister."

There was a square of brown paper tucked into the baby's blanket. Nettie knelt beside the basket and studied the paper. "It says something, but I don't know what," she said, and stood up. "You take one handle and I'll take the other, like on wash day," she said to Nellie.

———

"'My wife is dead, and I can't care for this, our dear baby, by myself. Do what you can for my little one, and show her the love I cannot,'" Nettie reported to the other girls that night in their beds. "That's what the note said. Matron read it out loud. Then she crumpled the paper up and burned it in the stove. All the baby had was that note, and Matron burned it.

"Just think," Nettie went on, "that baby won't remember anywhere but this place. She'll grow up right here, and live here, always. It'll be her forever home," she said with a glance at Nellie.

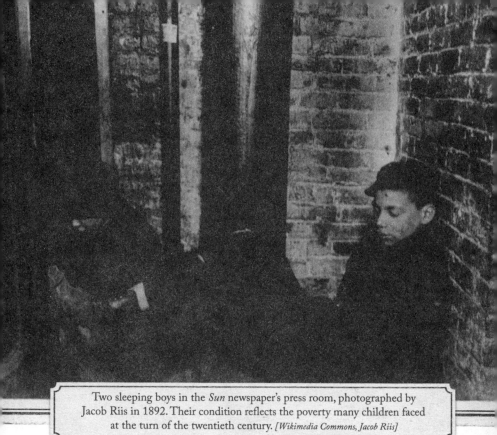

Two sleeping boys in the *Sun* newspaper's press room, photographed by Jacob Riis in 1892. Their condition reflects the poverty many children faced at the turn of the twentieth century. *[Wikimedia Commons, Jacob Riis]*

"Nobody lives here forever," said Bucky.

"Except Matron," Brenda added, and hid her smirk behind her hand.

"If you don't get a new family," Bucky said, "you live here till you're fourteen. Then it's good-bye, good luck, and don't let the door hit you on your way out."

Brenda blinked fast. "I'm going on fourteen now," she said. "My birthday's in November, not that they let me mark the day."

"Sever all ties," Nettie said, quoting the matron.

"Don't look back," said Nellie.

But Nettie couldn't help but look back. Every day, she wished for Mama and Father and Leon. Every day, she prayed for Sissy up in heaven. Every day, she could hardly tell anger from sadness.

And every day, though she tried very hard not to, she forgot them a little bit more. But just between themselves, she and Nellie called the basket-baby Sissy.

CHAPTER 7

September 11, 1911. The breakfast dishes were cleaned and put away, and Nellie and Nettie were taking off their aprons, when the matron bustled into the kitchen.

"Come along, step lively," said the matron. She began to tap some of the girls on the head. "You, and you," she said to two more of the girls on kitchen duty—Brenda O'Hare and Bucky. She tapped Nellie and Nettie. "Today's the day."

Nettie looked at Nellie. What day?

"Go to your room and change your clothes," the matron said, "then line up at the front door. Hurry, now. The dray wagon's already parked out front. I can hear Mr. Fry's horse stamping and snorting from here. I'll be glad to be rid of you, though more will surely come to take your place. . . ." Her voice faded as she marched out of the kitchen.

Nettie's hands shook as she put on the new dress Matron had put out on her bed, but she pretended she wasn't scared and confused. "She's not half as glad to be rid of us as we are to go," she said.

Nellie pulled Nettie aside. "But where are we going?" she whispered, her face pale. "Back to Mama, you think?"

"I don't think so, else why would the others be leaving, too?" Nettie whispered back. "We're going *together*, anyway."

Nellie smiled weakly.

"How do I look?" said Brenda O'Hare. "A proper lady, right?" She blew out her cheeks, puffing her red bangs.

The girls fairly tumbled down the stairs to the front door, where they stuffed their arms into their coat sleeves and lined up in front of the matron. Nettie and Nellie slipped their twin spoon dolls into their coat pockets.

They followed the matron out the door in a line, eight children in all—four girls, three boys, and the baby. Matron held the new baby in her arms and uncharacteristically cooed, then handed her over to the oldest girl, red-haired Brenda. "Don't bother anybody. Don't ask any questions. Be good as gold, or they'll send you straight back to me," she warned.

Mr. Fry helped the girls up into the wagon. "Hep, hep, there you go, Nettie."

Nettie grabbed Mr. Fry's sleeve. "Where are we going? Where are you taking us?"

"Kingston depot," he said. "I don't know where you're to go from there. Next stop, Kingston depot!"

The wagon pulled away. The big trees that had seemed like giants the day they came to the orphanage last winter were now full of leaves that were just beginning to turn colors. Their limbs seemed to wave good-bye.

Nettie waved to the big building before the wagon went around the corner. *Good-bye, Leon,* she thought. They had not seen him in nine months. She reckoned they'd never see him again.

⸺⊷≎≎⊶⸺

The children from the Kingston orphanage were not the only ones gathered in front of the depot. There must have been near twenty children in all.

"Think we ought to make a run for it?" said Brenda. She bounced the baby on her shoulder, patting the blanketed bundle awkwardly.

Nettie hoped Brenda wouldn't run. Whatever was going to happen, it had to be better than living in a box over a steam grate, the way Brenda had been doing before she came to live at the orphanage. Living in a box would be fun for a few days, like a bear in a cozy den, or a dog in a little doghouse. But not for very long.

"Children! Children, hello!" A woman approached along the walkway with purposeful strides that set her woolen cape swinging. She wore a matching navy-blue hat and carried a large leather handbag that looked sturdy enough to carry Father's tools.

"My name is Anna Laura Hill." Miss Hill smiled broadly. "And I am going to take you all on a trip. Would you like to take a ride on a train with me?"

Anna Laura Hill looked at the children standing before her. They were confused and frightened: some wore tough expressions; others shuffled their little feet and hugged themselves, as if no one else in the world cared enough to hug them. Anna Laura Hill had taken many such children on many such trains. She was an agent of the Children's Aid Society.

"Twins!" Miss Hill said in the direction of Nellie and Nettie. "How wonderful. When I was a girl, I used to pretend I had a twin sister. Someone I could *really* talk to."

Nettie had a hundred questions. Where would they go? How long would they be on the train? How long would they stay when they got wherever they were going? Did Mama know? She opened her mouth and took a big breath, but before she could speak, Nellie grabbed her hand and squeezed it. Her eyes were round as saucers and darting every which way. She was scared.

"I don't want to go back to the orphanage," Nellie whispered.

Nettie nodded. For her sister's sake, she swallowed her questions.

Miss Hill handed a badge to each child. Nettie could recognize her name and Nellie's, already printed in neat handwriting on their badges. They were also given a toothbrush, a change of clothes, and a comb. The clothes looked too large, but they were clean and fresh-smelling.

Miss Hill led them down the platform, where they boarded a train and sat where they were told, on a hard bench seat. It itched their legs where the horsehair stuffing poked out. Then they heard a shout—"Board! Alllllll aboard!"—and the train began to move. At first it seemed to leave their stomachs behind. It chugged and chuffed and picked up speed. Clouds of black smoke puffed past the windows. A whistle blew long and loud.

Miss Hill smiled at each and every one of the children in her care, and Nettie's nervous stomach settled

a bit. Wherever they were bound, it had to be better than the orphanage. But why wouldn't Miss Hill tell them where they were going?

Out the window, scenes flew by. Cityscapes became rolling hills, with small towns every so often. Nettie saw a red-and-white-striped circus tent set up by the tracks. "Look at that!" she said. But they went by too fast to see anything interesting. For a while, though, they passed the time imagining what wonders might have been inside that tent. Elephants? Acrobats? Clowns?

After some time, they stopped and ate sandwiches in a little town, and Miss Hill got the children some cold fresh milk. She fed and changed the baby herself, much to Brenda O'Hare's relief.

"Ugly little rotter," Brenda said.

Miss Hill smiled and put the baby up on her shoulder, patting her little back. "There, there," she murmured. Then she began to hum and, bending her knees, swayed gently side to side. "All children are beautiful, Brenda," she said, "including you."

Brenda flushed red but looked pleased.

Nettie thought of baby Sissy. "Do you have your own babies?" she said.

Miss Hill switched the baby to the other shoulder. "I'm not married," she said, "but I have many children in my life. I can't help but think of them all as a little bit my own."

"Is this where we're stopping, lady?" asked a boy who was about the twins' age. He spoke in a tough voice and wore his newsboy cap pushed back on his head—a cap like the one Leon used to wear when he worked selling papers. He acted rough, but the way the boy stuffed his hands in his pockets and shifted side to side in his boots made Nettie think he was as scared as she was. He came up just to the shoulder of a bigger boy who stood solidly beside him. He wasn't so tough that he minded holding his brother's hand when the bigger boy reached for it.

Miss Hill shook her head. "Not here, dear." She passed the baby back to Brenda, then looked at her papers. "Joe, is it?" The boy nodded. "Joe Wilson? And your big brother . . . let's see"—she checked the paper again—"Robert. Two wonderful brothers."

Robert Wilson frowned. "We never been apart, not ever, miss," he said.

"That's good, Robert," said Miss Hill. "People like to see siblings get along. Maybe someone will want two boys. Two nice brothers like you." A hooded look crossed her face—a look that seemed to mean "fingers crossed."

Miss Hill ushered the children back on board the railcar, and the train once more took off, west, and west, and still farther west, into the setting sun. Night fell. Everything was noisy, and dirty, and covered in black soot from the coal that the train engine burned. It was cold, too, and utterly dark. Nettie huddled beside Nellie under a blanket. A soft snore came from somewhere behind them, and Nettie thought of Father, and the times they'd all been together, all in one place. Mama, Father, Leon, Sissy. A family. She squeezed her eyes shut against the sadness, but the darkness was just the same.

"Are you awake?" Nettie felt more than heard her sister's whisper in her ear.

Nettie nodded, their heads touching against the back of the hard seat. Nellie drew out her spoon doll. "We are six now. Maybe we're too big for stories. But—I think Dolly would like to hear one," she said softly.

"Okay." Nettie didn't even poke fun at Dolly's dumb name. She pulled out her twin spoon doll, Min, and thought of Mama, making all the tiny stitches in the doll's calico dress. Nettie felt a sob choking her. She cleared her throat. "Once upon a time," she murmured, "there were twin princesses, as fair as fairies, maybe not really as gentle as lambs, but as strong and true as an oxen team."

There was no answering *bahhhh* or *moooo* this time from Nellie, only a little sniffling. "Those twin princesses were locked up in the witch's castle, but then they snuck out. And in the dark of night, they climbed up onto a dragon's back. That dragon was asleep in the woods, and when he woke up, he couldn't even feel them there on his scaly back. He huffed and chuffed and black smoke came out of his nose, but those two princesses just held on tight and rode far away from the castle and the witch and the woods."

Nellie sniffled again, and Nettie could tell she was trying not to cry. "I'm scared," Nellie said. "Where are they taking us? Why won't they tell us?"

Nettie thought she could hear the newsboy, Joe, crying a few seats away, and she heard his big brother Robert's soothing voice, though she couldn't make out the words.

Nettie gripped Min tight in one hand and put her other arm around her sister. "Well, we're on our way. Wherever they take us, we'll stick together," she said.

Nettie tucked the blanket under Nellie's chin. Because everyone knows, twin princesses in stories always take care of each other. Nettie hoped Miss Hill knew that, too.

CHAPTER 8

In the morning, the train gave a great final *chug* and *sigh*, and stopped. All the children stepped out onto the platform. This was Union Station in Kansas City. Nettie had butterflies in her stomach. Big ones.

Another sign was posted beneath the station sign.

"'Homes wanted,'" Robert read, looking hard at the sign. "'For children.'"

Those butterflies flapped wildly now. The children all turned to Miss Hill.

"Are we gonna get new families?" Robert asked. He put his hands on his little brother's shoulders.

Robert must not be afraid of being sent back to some

Union Station in Kansas City, Missouri—the first stop on the twins' trip west. This photograph was taken sometime between 1910 and 1930. *[LC-D419-132]*

matron for asking questions, Nettie thought, with a glance at Nellie.

"Children," Miss Hill said, "I thought it best not to tell you. You've been through so much already, I didn't want to upset you. The Children's Aid Society is sponsoring your placing-out with new families." She smiled brightly. "We know of families who want children just like you. Here in Missouri, and in other states, too." She pointed to the sign. "People will come," she said.

"Farming families, good folks with enough room in their houses and their hearts."

Miss Hill explained that the families promised to treat the orphans like family. They'd be expected to work, just as family members work. They'd go to school, and to church on Sundays. Catholic children would be placed with Catholic families, Protestant with Protestant, and so on, to make as close a match as possible.

"You'll have mothers and fathers," she went on. Her voice was tender. "Brothers and sisters, maybe. It's a bright day, boys and girls," she said. "A very bright day indeed."

Nettie wanted to believe her. She elbowed Nellie with more enthusiasm than she felt. "See? It'll be okay," she said.

Before long, people came. There were shopkeepers and carpenters, blacksmiths and farmers. There was a lady with a green-sprigged bonnet and a cruel-looking walking stick. A tall, stooped man with a stern chin. Most of the faces were thin with hollow, weather-reddened cheeks and pale eyes peering from under brows bleached by the sun.

A friendly-looking couple stood close together with their shoulders touching. The lady blinked back tears, looking around at the children who'd come all this way on the train to find families to love. *They would be good parents*, Nettie thought, and she let herself hope, just a little.

The nice couple wasn't there two minutes before they selected the baby and walked away. Nettie felt a sharp pang, watching their pretend baby sister go away with her pretend parents. She knew that the baby would never remember them. And the nice couple hadn't even glanced at Nettie and Nellie.

The placing-out day wasn't as "bright" as Miss Hill had said it would be. Not all of the people seemed like "good folks."

"Pull up your skirts. Lemme see your legs ain't crooked," the green-bonnet lady said to Bucky.

Nettie held her breath. Bucky was likely to scowl and talk back at someone who spoke to her like that. But she was astonished when Bucky smiled wide and showed her knees. "Straight and strong," Bucky said proudly. "I ain't even knock-kneed!"

"Hmph," went the lady in the bonnet. Then she

nodded once, satisfied, and thumped her walking stick. "Spirited, this one," she said to Miss Hill. "Looks good and strong, and I like a gal with some vinegar in her."

"I got some vinegar in me," said Nettie. Nellie frowned at her and shook her head.

Bucky went away with the woman, with only one little wave back at the rest of the children. Maybe she didn't dare look back again, Nettie thought. Maybe she didn't want to say good-bye.

The tall, stooped man was looking Robert Wilson up and down. He gripped Robert's upper arm to measure his muscle. Robert stood straighter and elbowed his little brother in the ribs. "Take off your cap, Joe," he whispered.

The stooped man hitched his belt and pointed at Robert. "That's the one for us," he told Miss Hill. "My wife and I lost six children, and we need a healthy one to work the farm."

"Come on, Joe," Robert said, and began to follow the man.

The man stopped and put up a hand. "Just you," he said to Robert. "I don't need the little one."

Robert's brow knotted. He looked at Miss Hill.

"It's the both of us," he said. "We never have been apart, Joe and me, in all this time."

But the man would not be moved to take Joe, and Robert had no choice but to go with him. It was better that one of them go to a new home than for both of them to risk having to return on the train to life in an orphanage.

"I'll find you, Joe," Robert said fiercely. "One day, I'll find you."

Miss Hill put her arm around Joe, who was crying as hard as anybody could cry, and trying just as hard not to. Nettie and Nellie knew what it was like not to be able to stop the tears from coming.

"I'm sorry, Joe," said Miss Hill. She unsnapped her handbag and took out a clean white handkerchief. "I can't promise to keep siblings together," she said, pressing the handkerchief into Joe's hand. "We do the best we can with the placing-out, but some folks only want one child."

Joe blew his nose miserably. Nettie looked at Nellie. Would they be split up, too?

"Can't we—can't we wait a minute?" Joe could barely get the words out. "Why does he have to go with that one?"

Miss Hill shook her head. "No, Joe. All the families are approved by the local people who help us find homes. That's the most we can do. If we pick and choose, we'll never find families for all the children who need them. We have so *many* children to place out."

Joe looked around, at Nellie and Nettie, at Brenda and the rest. "So many children?" he said. His eyes were frantic, his face blotchy and streaked. "But there's not that many of us," he said, gulping back tears. "I don't know what you mean!" He drew his coat sleeve under his dripping nose.

"This isn't the only orphan train, Joe," said Miss Hill. Again, she unsnapped her handbag and rooted around until she found what she was looking for. "Look at this picture," she said, showing them. "This is Henry, and here is June, and Peter," she said, pointing at the small faces in the photograph. "That one's Bonny." She smiled fondly, then tucked the picture back into her bag and snapped it shut. "You and Robert are two orphans," Miss Hill went on, "two among thousands. That's right, Joe. This train is but one of many such trains coming west."

Orphan train. It was the first time Nettie had heard the words, but it would not be the last.

Miss Hill settled Joe on one end of a bench, where he sat crying, his cap pressed to his eyes. She told Nellie and Nettie to sit at the other end of the bench, and so they did.

"Sing something pretty," she encouraged them. "People will come and see what wonderful children you are."

Nettie didn't want to sing in front of these strangers. She didn't want the people looking at them, asking them to lift their skirts to see if their legs were crooked, like the lady who took Bucky.

"Sing 'Jesus Loves Me,'" Miss Hill prompted. She hummed a little, to get the girls started.

> *"Jesus loves me, this I know*
> *For the Bible tells me so*
> *Little ones to Him belong*
> *They are weak but He is strong."*

A man and a woman stepped close, listening. The lady tilted her head and rested it gently on the man's shoulder. When the song was over, she clapped.

Nettie held Nellie's hand, and they sat very still. *Be good as gold*, Matron had said. The lady and the

man looked nice. They held hands the way Mama and
Father used to, sometimes. What would happen now?

The lady spoke to Miss Hill. Miss Hill glanced at
them and bit her lip. Then she shook her head no. The
man leaned in and said something, and again Miss
Hill shook her head. The people walked away.

"Didn't they like our singing?" Nellie asked Miss
Hill.

"They liked your singing very much, Nellie," said
Miss Hill. "But they only want one child."

Nettie looked at poor Joe Wilson. He had stopped sobbing, but his shoulders still shook from it, and his breaths came in short gasps, the way Sissy's used to after a bad fit.

"You told them no?" said Nettie.

Miss Hill glanced at Joe, and nodded. "I told them no," she said.

CHAPTER 9

Nellie and Nettie were not chosen that day. Joe Wilson, too, was still on the orphan train as it pulled out of Kansas City, and so was Brenda O'Hare.

"Nobody wants a red-haired girl," Brenda said as the train rolled on. She stared out the window at the flat landscape. "And I'm older than they like, too," she said. "I wonder what's going to happen to me if I don't get picked. If I have to go back." Brenda's chin trembled, and she looked up at the luggage rack to keep the tears in her eyes from falling. She knew very well what often became of girls who were too old for the orphanages and had nowhere to go.

Nettie stared out the window and thought about

what they'd left behind, and what they might find out here, out west. Miss Hill moved around here and there on the railcar to keep company with the children. Then she sat beside Brenda, across from Nettie and Nellie, pulled yarn and needles from her bag, and began to knit. The knitting needles quietly clicked, as if whispering to the clacking train.

"I'd sure like to see a buffalo out the window," Nettie said.

"Buffalo?" Miss Hill dropped her knitting in her lap.

Nellie nodded. "Like the song goes."

"Ah," said Miss Hill, nodding and picking up a dropped stitch. "I see. No, I'm afraid all the buffalo are gone."

Nettie looked out the window again and sighed. Then she heard a pretty sound. It was Miss Hill, and she was humming. Soon the humming turned to singing, a soft voice that made Nettie think of Mama.

"Oh give me a home, where the buffalo roam, where the deer and the antelope play," sang Miss Hill. She smiled and then went on, and Brenda wiped her cheeks and joined her song.

"Where seldom is heard, a discouraging word, and the skies are not cloudy all day."

Nettie leaned her head back against the hard seat and closed her eyes, listening to Miss Hill's song. She must have snoozed, because she woke to the sound of the train conductor's voice.

"Apples!" he sang out. "Apples for you." He walked down the aisle through the railcar, pausing at every seat so each rider could choose an apple.

Nettie dug eagerly through the crate to find a good one. "But they're all crawling with worms!" she wailed.

"Right you are, little lady!" said the conductor. "Throw 'em out the windows, kids," he said. "Throw 'em all out there. We'll have apple trees blooming all along the tracks someday. Everybody will know you were here."

Nettie threw apple after apple out the window and watched each one bounce and roll. It felt good to throw the apples, as if she was throwing her sad, scared feelings out the window and watching them roll away. But as soon as the apples were gone, her bad feelings rolled right back in.

Nettie slept deeply that night, lulled by the endless clacking rhythm of the train. She dreamed she and Nellie were in a place with apple trees all around, apple trees as far as she could see. There was a ladder leaned up against a tree, and Nettie began to climb. Up and up among the branches she went, till she could no longer see the ground. Nellie was gone now. She was alone, high in the tree. Twigs scratched her face, and there was scurrying and scrabbling around her, but no matter how quickly she turned her head, she couldn't see whatever was up in the tree with her. It wasn't Nellie. Nellie was no longer there. A sudden blaring noise startled her. She clung to a branch as the tree began to sway and lurch. She held on with all her might, but the shaking and swaying became more violent. The tree shook so hard she couldn't hold on. She lost her grip and fell down, down. Many voices called out as she fell: *Nobody will know you were here, nobody will know you were here, nobody will know you. . . .*

Nettie woke with a start, chilled and breathing hard. There was Nellie, beside her on the bench seat in the pitch-black night. Carefully, so as not to wake Nellie, she sat up and pulled the blanket up under her chin. She wondered what time it was, and how much night was left. She looked out the window and watched the darkness for a sign the dawn was coming.

⊸⊶⊷⊷⊶⊸

Their next stop was in a town the conductor told them was McPherson, in Kansas. They stepped out onto the platform, as they had done in Kansas City, Missouri.

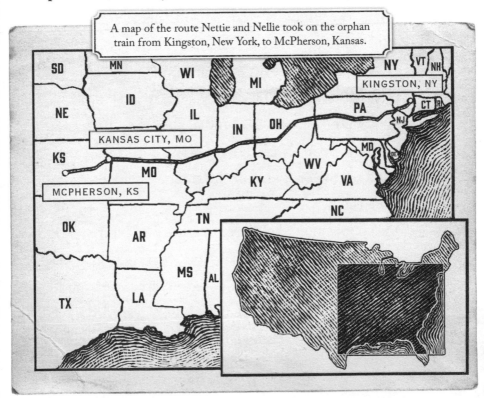

A map of the route Nettie and Nellie took on the orphan train from Kingston, New York, to McPherson, Kansas.

This depot was even busier and more crowded with people coming and going. Everyone seemed to have important business.

The business of finding a forever home was important, too.

The September air felt heavy that day as Miss Hill led the children straight up to the big doors of a great brick building.

"This place—it makes me think of the day we went to the orphanage," Nellie said to Nettie, and took her hand. It had been a different season then. Now it was hot and sticky. Their dresses clung to the backs of their legs. Their collars grabbed at their throats.

Nettie followed Nellie inside. The great sloped hall was lined with rows of seats, and at the front, there was a stage. It was the opera house, Miss Hill told them. She lined up the orphans on the stage, where everyone could see them.

One couple looked closely at Nellie and Nettie. The woman stood square and squat, and even though it was hot, she wore a dark-colored sweater across her round shoulders. Her face was flat and her eyes drooped. Nettie thought she looked just like a bulldog. She knew she shouldn't think such a mean thing, and so she smiled as nicely as she could, to make up for her unkind thoughts. *Good as gold*, she thought, *good as gold*.

The man stood a few paces behind his wife. He was a portly fellow with cheeks reddened—Nettie hoped by a jolly nature. But he couldn't be very jolly, she thought, for his eyes were watery, and his chin dropped away under his mouth, and he twisted his hat in his hands.

The bulldog lady adjusted her eyeglasses and looked again at the twins, up and down, as if inspecting them for bugs or dirt. Nettie knew they were clean. Miss Hill made sure of that.

Nellie and Nettie held hands, even though Miss Hill told them not to. Nettie remembered how poor Joe cried when they took his big brother away, and she held on tight to Nellie.

"We'll take 'em," said the woman.

Nettie looked anxiously at Nellie, and then at Miss Hill.

"Both," said the man. He gave the girls a quick smile and glanced at his wife. "We'll take them both."

Nellie and Nettie said a quick good-bye to Joe Wilson and Brenda O'Hare. They hadn't known Joe for long, but Nettie was sad to say good-bye, and she hoped he'd be reunited with Robert someday. It was hard to leave Brenda—red-haired, bighearted Brenda—after so many months together at the orphanage.

"Good-bye, Brenda," Nettie said.

"We hope you find a nice family," said Nellie.

"Don't worry about me," she told them. "A street rat always finds a way to get by." She smiled and gave a cheerful little wave, but her chin trembled and she turned away.

They were sad, too, to leave Miss Hill. She had seemed to care.

———————

The bulldog lady was named Gertie Chapin. The portly, red-cheeked man was her husband, L. F. Chapin. Mr. Chapin owned a grocery store in a small town called Canton. They were a childless couple, and Mrs. Chapin said she needed help around the house.

"Dainty little things, aren't you," she said to the girls. Her voice sounded mean, as if she thought the twins weren't good for much. Nettie swallowed hard. She wanted Mrs. Chapin to like them.

"We're six," said Nettie, "and we know how to scrub

floors, and dust the tabletops, and change the sheets, and beat the rugs."

"We're strong as an oxen team," Nellie piped up. She did not say *mooooo*.

Mrs. Chapin turned to them, her bulldog face as blank as a pie pan. "We'll see," she said.

It took all day long in the horse-and-buggy to get to Canton, Kansas. Mostly, they were quiet and watched the scenery go by. They had never seen so many cows. And the clouds! The land was so flat and the sky was so big and blue that the clouds had plenty of room to make themselves into interesting shapes.

"Elephant," Nellie whispered, pointing.

"Fancy hat with a feather," said Nettie. A vision of the mysterious aunt came into her mind, and she pushed it away.

Finally, Mr. Chapin drove into a town and down a wide, straight street lined with one- and two-story buildings.

"That there's my grocery store," Mr. Chapin said, pointing to a corner building with an awning over the window. He turned to the girls and smiled. Nettie thought of the kind grocer, Mr. DiSopo, who had cried at the side of Sissy's coffin.

A grocery store in Kansas from the early twentieth century. *[LC-USF33-T01-001235-M2]*

Mr. Chapin drove the buggy through the short stretch of buildings that was the town center and out the other side, then farther along to a white clapboard house with a gabled porch, the posts and ornamented trim painted gray like a pigeon.

"This is it," said Mrs. Chapin.

"Home, sweet home," said Mr. Chapin. "Welcome, Nellie," he said. "Welcome, Nettie." His watery eyes looked straight at each twin when he said her name, and he didn't mix them up, even though they looked almost exactly alike! "Gertie and I"—he glanced at his wife's back as she stomped up the walk—"well, we're mighty glad to have you." He winked.

Nettie gave him a quick smile. Mrs. Chapin didn't seem very friendly, but maybe Mr. Chapin would make up for it.

CHAPTER 10

Mrs. Chapin showed the girls upstairs to their room, which was small and tidy, wallpapered in a delicate repeating floral. A wardrobe stood along one wall, and against another was a set of twin beds with matching white bedspreads. Between the beds was a window that faced west into the setting sun and overlooked the backyard, and beneath the window stood a small table.

Mrs. Chapin tugged the curtain closed. "We'll have a cold supper shortly. Settle in." She looked them up and down, as she had done back on that stage in McPherson, before choosing them like a couple of kittens from a cardboard box. "Wash your hands and faces," she said. "I can't abide dirt." Then she turned and left them in their room.

Their room! Mrs. Chapin's manner was rough, and Nettie didn't like her. But she liked their room so much she threw her arms around Nellie and burst into tears she had long held back. No more dormitory room. No more orphan train.

"We'll be happy here, won't we?" Nellie said.

"Sure thing," Nettie said. "They didn't split us up, like poor old Joe and Robert Wilson. We'll be happy, all right."

They both took out Min and Dolly and propped them on their pillows. Then they washed up and went downstairs for supper.

That first night in their new home, Nettie didn't mind that supper had been a mostly silent meal. They ate. How they ate! There were cooked carrots and canned green beans in a divided dish with two bowls. There was a plate of cold sliced beef. There was a loaf of sliced white bread, and nobody stopped them from spreading each slice thick with sweet butter. When they finished one glass of cold milk, they were allowed another, filled almost to the brim.

"I don't know how they fed you in that orphanage, but here in a civilized home, we don't eat with our elbows on the table like that," said Mrs. Chapin.

The girls were used to protecting their supper from reaching arms by hunching over their food. Nellie flushed red and put her hands in her lap.

Mrs. Chapin continued to do the talking while Mr. Chapin slowly chewed, and what she talked about was rules.

"'There's a right way of doing things, and a wrong way,'" Nellie quoted Mrs. Chapin as the girls lay in their beds that night, the window open above the little table between them to welcome some cooler night air.

"I bet there's lots more than *one* wrong way," Nettie said, "and I hope old Gertie Chapin won't point out every single one." She rested her hands on her full belly. They had already found out that the wrong way to clear the dinner dishes was to stack the plates at the table. They were to carry plates one by one to the sink so they wouldn't break anything.

Nellie burped. "Excuse me," she said, and they both giggled.

"No belching at the table, idiot girl!" said Nettie, wagging a finger like Mrs. Chapin.

Mrs. Chapin had explained how she liked the cleaning done, and the wash, and the gardening. It sounded like hard work. But she would see that they were hard workers. They would show her she'd picked the right girls for her family.

"Tell me a story," said Nellie. She climbed out of her bed and into Nettie's.

Nettie heaved a great yawn, but she nodded. "Once upon a time," Nettie said, "there were two little twin princesses, as fair as fairies, as gentle as lambs, more or less, and as strong and true as an oxen team." Nettie yawned again. "And the twin princesses always took care of each other, and all that."

Nellie nodded.

"We already know they got away from the witch's castle on the back of a dragon. Well, next thing you know, the dragon lifted up off the ground! The princesses held on for dear life, and it wasn't too bad. It was nice to look at the world from far away, where nobody could get their hands on them. But then the dragon flew down and started breathing fire, so the princesses had to think fast. They slid off the dragon's back, quick as they could."

"Did they fall far?" Nellie asked sleepily.

"Not too far," said Nettie. "And they landed in a big pile of hay."

"That was lucky," said Nellie.

A knock came at the door. "Quiet down, now," came Mrs. Chapin's voice. "Morning comes early around here!" Nettie was glad she didn't open the door. She might have made them get in their own beds, like the matron had always tried to do at the orphanage.

The very next minute, it seemed, there was another knock at the door. Coming abruptly out of sleep, Nettie thought it was the man with the papers, coming again to take them away from Mama.

"I don't know how late they let you sleep in at the orphanage," Mrs. Chapin scolded, her bulldog cheeks rippling with agitation, "and heaven only knows what behavior your neglectful parents taught you, but from here on out, you'll be up early."

Nettie yawned and rubbed her eyes. "We got up at five every day," she said.

"Don't you talk back to me," said Mrs. Chapin.

"I was only saying we're early ris—"

Mrs. Chapin's glare shut Nettie up.

Nettie and Nellie scrambled into their clothes and down the stairs. It was too bad that Mr. Chapin had gone to the store for the day and left them alone with Mrs. Chapin. They sat at the table and tucked into the bowls of gluey oatmeal she'd put out.

"Are we going to school today?" Nellie asked. "Miss Hill said we'd be going to school."

"You'll go to school when I say so, but we've got other plans for today."

Mrs. Chapin's plan, it soon became clear, was for the girls to do the washing. Mr. Chapin's shirts and collars were sent out to the commercial laundry in town. "But linens and personals we do here," she told them. Washing was a two-person job that took all day and required the help of a washerwoman. "Now I've got the pair of you, I got no need of her," said Mrs. Chapin.

"I never trusted that woman. I know she stole my pewter bud vase."

Breakfast over, Mrs. Chapin set the girls to work. First, they lugged buckets of water from the well behind the house. Full buckets were too heavy, so they quickly learned to fill them halfway.

"I'll race you!" said Nettie. Even half full, the buckets were heavy. By the fourth trip, the race wasn't any fun. Nettie's arms felt stretched thin like rubber bands already, and they hadn't even begun to do the washing. They'd worked on washing day plenty of times back at the orphanage, but there had been many hands to help, some of them older and bigger girls like Bucky and Brenda. Here, it was just the two of them.

Mrs. Chapin heated the water while the girls carried more and more buckets from the well. They put the wash in the water and began to stir the clothes with a long stick. Then they scrubbed against a washboard every item of clothing, every inch of every sheet and heavy towel. The coarse lye soap burned their hands. Hours ticked by.

Once the scrubbing was done, it was time to boil the clothes. Nettie's arm still bore a scar from the time

she'd burned it on the radiator, and so she was careful to keep clear of the boiling-hot water. She took turns with Nellie, stirring the clothes in the tub to make sure they didn't catch on the bottom and scorch. Once the laundry was fully boiled, they had to drag the heavy items out of the hot water with a wash stick. Nettie thought her rubber-band arms would snap, and her back, too.

"Now you need a tub of clear water for the rinsing," Mrs. Chapin said.

Nettie and Nellie dragged their feet out to the pump.

"It's like starting all over again," Nellie said, working the pump handle up and down. "I want to lie down right here on the ground."

The squeak of the pump handle grated on Nettie's nerves like the constant wail of baby Sissy, right before Mama would lose her temper and start to yell. She gritted her teeth.

"You can do it," Nettie said. "You have to. We both have to." She glanced back toward the house. "You see how she keeps watching us? She's just waiting for us to fall down dead our very first day here, and we won't."

"I can't. Nettie, I just can't." Tears filled Nellie's eyes.

"You can," said Nettie. "You got to. Now, come on." She knew she sounded sharp, but Nellie couldn't quit on her. She just couldn't.

Nettie hauled her bucket toward the house and prayed Nellie would follow her. She didn't know what would happen if Gertie Chapin found them sitting down or quitting, but it would be something bad. A moment later, she heard Nellie stumbling behind her.

They filled the tub with clean water.

They rinsed the clothes.

More buckets. More water.

They hauled water to rinse the clothes once more, this time with bluing.

"Now wring them out, good and dry," said Mrs. Chapin.

They had to wring every bit of wash by hand, twisting and squeezing.

Heavy, heavy.

Nettie hung her head, too exhausted to speak. Too weak to rise from her knees. "There," she breathed, at last. Her knuckles were rough and red and peeling. She sucked on the side of her thumb where the skin bled and stung. Her back and neck ached as if someone held a hot poker between her shoulder blades.

But the laundry was, all of it, clean. Finally, finally, they were finished. The sun was low. It had been the longest day Nettie could remember in her life. She smiled at Nellie. "All done," she said. "We did it."

Nellie nodded, but barely. She did not raise her gaze to Nettie's. She didn't manage a smile.

Nettie heard the clomp of Mrs. Chapin's shoes and turned her head slowly to look up at her. "Done," she said.

Mrs. Chapin turned her bulldog face to Nettie and looked at her a long moment. "Not quite. Go and hang the clothes out." She turned and walked away.

Nellie lowered her head to the edge of the tub. Nettie could see her shoulders shaking.

Slowly, Nettie got on her hands and knees, then rose to her feet. She started to drag the clothes basket. It was too heavy to lift. A moment later, Nellie got up and began to push the basket from the other side, and together they pulled and pushed it to the clothesline

Laundry hanging on a clothesline.
[LC-USF34-039476-D]

beside the house. Nellie tugged at a twist of wet cloth. Unexpectedly, it came free of the tangle of clothes and flopped onto the dirt.

Mrs. Chapin was there in an instant—like a spider, patient and deadly quick.

"Idiot girl!" She raised her hand and slapped Nellie full across the face. Nellie cried out. Nettie, enraged, flew to Mrs. Chapin and began to beat her small fists into her soft stomach. Mrs. Chapin grabbed hold of Nettie's wrists and held them tightly. Nettie tossed her head like a frightened horse.

"Don't you hit my sister!" Nettie yelled. Nellie was crying, hiding her face in her hands.

Mrs. Chapin flung Nettie to the ground and stood there, panting and red-faced. She pointed at the laundry. "You did it wrong. Do it again." Her voice sounded like the growl of a mean dog, the kind you hope's tied up.

Nettie rubbed her wrists where they hurt. "It's only one measly apron," she said. "We'll fix it. We'll just shake the dirt off it. I'll rinse it off."

Mrs. Chapin's lips went white. "Don't you sass me," she said. Slowly, she leaned over, took hold of the edge of the basket, and toppled the clean clothes—every last thing—onto the dirt.

Nettie stared at Gertie Chapin's brown lace-up shoes. Why were some people so hard and cruel? Why would anybody be?

The shoes moved away. "Do it right this time."

CHAPTER 11

After three days with Gertie Chapin, the girls were thrilled when Mr. Chapin took them to work at the store. The store was one big room, with a high ceiling and long wooden counters. On one end of the counter was a great glass urn packed full of pickled vegetables, with a Heinz label pasted to the glass. There was a big scale to measure out goods. There were sacks of flour and sugar, crates of apples and pears. The big-bellied woodstove in the center of the room pumped out heat in waves, but it was cooler at the edges of the room and in the corner where there was a bucket of small whisk brooms and a barrel of tall straw kitchen brooms.

The interior of a Midwestern grocery store.
[LC-USF34-030429-D]

Mr. Chapin was pulling a crisp white apron over his head and tying it around his ample middle when the little bell above the door rang, announcing the first customer of the day. Mr. Chapin stepped right up to the counter. "Good morning, Mr. Neumann," he said. "What can I do you for today?"

Mr. Neumann wanted some canned goods and some fresh fruit and a bag of Chase & Sanborn's coffee, and Mr. Chapin collected the items for him while the customer waited, smiling pleasantly at Nellie and Nettie while they busied themselves attacking the store's many shelves with a feather duster.

"That there's choicest private growth coffee beans," said Mr. Chapin as he handed the sack of groceries to Mr. Neumann. He was proud to be able to offer his customers the finest goods available, even if his wife was stingy with the same items at home. "Sell it, don't waste it," she'd say, if he brought her something decent

The layout of a typical grocery store in the early twentieth century. *[LC-USZ62-114699]*

from the store. He glanced at the twins. *Daughters! Maybe Gertie will loosen up,* he thought, with children in the house. Maybe she'd be a little softer now.

Mr. Neumann left, and the girls climbed up a ladder to line up rows of cans, three cans high and five cans deep. Then he had them put up the signs he'd hand-lettered. He had such pretty handwriting! Canned peaches were twenty-five cents a can, or six for a dollar thirty-eight. There were cans of pineapple for twenty cents each, or six for a dollar and ten cents, and canned corn and canned cherries and plums. Peas for twelve cents a can, or six for seventy cents. The rows of cans went on and on. So much food!

There were baskets hung on nails all around the store, marked with prices that ranged from twenty cents to a dollar. Nettie imagined them filled with colored eggs and candy, come Easter time—Hershey's Silvertops and peanut butter Peach Blossoms, her favorite, and paper-wrapped rolls of Necco wafers.

Mr. Chapin seemed to enjoy having the girls help. He kept smiling, and his reddened cheeks looked as merry as old Saint Nick's.

"Your spoon dolls could be great friends with the feather dusters!" he suggested. Then he put a bonnet

on a straw broom and danced with "her," all around the store. The girls laughed till their sides ached, and they did not miss Mrs. Gertrude Chapin one bit.

The little bell above the door chimed, and in came a woman with a boy in tow.

Mr. Chapin set his straw-faced dance partner aside, pulled a square handkerchief from his back pocket, and patted his brow. "Why, hello, there, Mrs. Coffin," he said, still chuckling.

The girls quickly set their feather dusters and spoon dolls on a shelf and snapped to attention. When she saw the boy wearing a newsboy cap, standing in Mrs. Coffin's shadow, Nettie's jaw dropped.

It was Joe Wilson! Joe, the boy who had been on the orphan train with them, and who'd been separated from his older brother, Robert. Nettie had not forgotten how poor Joe sobbed on the train platform as he watched his big brother walk away, and how she and Nellie were allowed to stay together.

"Joe! Joe Wilson!" Nettie couldn't keep the pleasure and surprise from her voice. Joe looked at them, then just as quickly looked away.

"Joe, it's us!" Nettie waved her hands and waggled her fingers to get his attention, as if he hadn't seen them. "From the train!" It was impossible that he didn't recognize them. All their lives, people had noticed the identical twin sisters. And it had been only a matter of days since they parted.

But here Joe was acting like he didn't know them at all. He glanced again their way, and then at Mrs. Coffin, who held tight to his hand. Then he stared down at his boots.

"This here is my nephew, *Will*," said Mrs. Coffin

deliberately, "my brother's boy. *Will Coffin*," she said, jerking the boy's hand, "say hello to Mr. Chapin."

"Pleased to meet you," the boy mumbled.

"Happy to make your acquaintance, Young Master Coffin," said Mr. Chapin. "The twins here are mistaken, aren't you, girls?" He looked at them as if he wanted them to agree, so they did.

"Yessir."

Nettie looked sidelong at Nellie. That boy sure was Joe Wilson. Why was everybody pretending he wasn't?

CHAPTER 12

On Sunday morning, at the breakfast table, Mrs. Chapin declared a day of rest.

"Thank the Lord," Nettie muttered.

Mr. Chapin chuckled.

"Indeed, Sunday is the Lord's day," said Mrs. Chapin with a glare at Mr. Chapin. "The Lord does not appreciate your disrespectful tone, Nettie, and neither do I."

Nettie opened her eyes wide to look innocent and sweet, like her doll, Min. "I'm Nellie," she said. *Blink-blink.*

Nellie hid her smile with her napkin, and Nettie

kicked her under the table to keep her from laughing.

Mrs. Chapin tilted her head very slightly and snuck looks at Nellie and Nettie. "Are you trying to play me?" she said.

"No, ma'am," said Nellie.

"No, we sure never have any fun with you," Nettie said, and then realized her mistake.

Mrs. Chapin's bulldog face went red. She grabbed the thing closest to hand, the doll Min, and cracked Nettie on the head with her.

"Ow!" said Nettie.

"You watch your tone," said Mrs. Chapin. She shoved the spoon doll into her handbag.

When it was time, they went to church. Nellie and Nettie listened carefully and tried to pay attention to the minister's sermon. Mrs. Chapin was watching. Whenever their eyes wandered, she'd rap the girls' hands on the knuckles with Min's wooden head.

Reverend Beebe droned on, reading out of the big Bible on the stand. "'Say not, I will do so to him as he hath done to me: I will render to the man according to his work.'" He raised his eyebrows, then looked down at the Bible again. "'Avenge not yourselves,'" he went on, "'but rather give place unto wrath: for it is written, Vengeance is mine; I will repay, saith the Lord.'"

After the sermon was over and the recessional hymn sung out, Mr. Chapin introduced the girls to Reverend Beebe, who greeted them warmly, in spite of all his talk about vengeance and wrath. He suggested the twins play with his daughter, Abigail, and son, Henry, during fellowship hour.

"You're orphans, right?" Abigail Beebe said. The minister's daughter considered them both, head to toe. She squinched up her face like she was smelling something bad.

"No." Nettie stuck out her chin and shoved her hands in the patch pockets of her dress. "Our mama and father aren't dead."

"If they're not dead, then why'd they send you way out here on the orphan train?" said Abigail's brother, Henry. "Don't they want you anymore? You must have done something evil to make them get rid of you like that."

Nettie felt like slugging both Beebes. But Mrs. Chapin kept glowering at them every so often, and she'd warned them to be good.

"How old are you?" Abigail wanted to know.

"Six." Nellie held out six fingers.

"Huh. I can't tell you one from the other, so how 'bout I just call you both Pig." Abigail tilted her head and smiled, like she was saying something friendly instead of something mean. Nettie narrowed her eyes.

"You steal stuff, Pig?" Abigail reached out and flicked the big bow on top of Nellie's head. "Orphans are dirty. Papa says you came out here with nothing but the clothes on your backs. I bet you stole those hair ribbons, Pig."

Now Abigail had gone too far. Nettie balled her hands into fists. "We never stole anything, Abigail Beebe! We never did!"

Nettie's shout drew the attention of Mrs. Chapin. She clutched her handbag, with poor Min stuffed inside, and marched toward the children. But the minister got there first. Nettie was so mad she couldn't look at Reverend Beebe. He'd probably see *wrath* written all over her face. She stared at the white square of his collar and pressed her fists to her sides.

"Abigail, Henry," he said to his children, "I trust you're making our brand-new neighbors welcome?"

"Of course, Papa," Abigail said sweetly.

"Just so, just so," said the minister, smiling and patting Nellie and Nettie on the tops of their heads.

Nettie ducked out from under Reverend Beebe's hand. She was so mad she could spit. For minister's kids, these two surely were mean. Nettie and Nellie had never been made to feel this bad in all their months at the orphanage, and here this was *church*!

⊶⊷⊶⊷

Back at home after church, the afternoon grew warm, and Mrs. Chapin rested on the couch with her stocking-feet up. It was too hot to be upstairs, so the girls sat in the kitchen, playing the silent game with their spoon dolls. The first one who made any noise lost. So far, they were both winning, and it wasn't much fun. Every so often Mrs. Chapin's light, rhythmic snoring from the other room was interrupted by a snort.

"What say we get out of here, girls?" said Mr. Chapin, very quietly. He pointed to the next room. "We'll just let her sleep," he said.

They followed Mr. Chapin outside. The door closed behind them with a quiet click.

"You girls know how to ride a bicycle?" Mr. Chapin asked. His watery eyes managed to twinkle.

"No, sir!" said Nellie.

"We can sure skip rope, though," Nettie added.

He led them to the small barn behind the house and slid the big door open. Inside was a bicycle, painted bright red.

"I hung it on wires from the rafters at the store, a special display," said Mr. Chapin, "but it never sold."

Children posed with tricycles and a bicycle, sometime between 1910 and 1920. *[LC-DIG-det-4a25886]*

He raked his fingers through his thinning hair. "Mrs. Chapin called it a waste of money, but I'm glad I kep' it," he said. "I must've known I'd have two little girls one day. Give it a spin," he offered.

Nettie went first. She climbed on. Even with Mr. Chapin holding on, the bicycle wobbled and teetered.

"Whoa, this is scary!"

"Okay, now you just hold on here, and sit tall, and I'll get the bike moving." Mr. Chapin held on to the seat and the handlebars, and jogged beside her down the earthen ramp of the barn. "I've got you," he was saying all along. She could feel his hand steadying the seat. The bicycle was wobbling, but she was holding on.

"I'm steering!"

"You're doing it!"

She turned too hard and the bike zagged, but Mr. Chapin corrected it. Nettie kept going down the earthen ramp and along the drive beside the house and out to the road, and she pedaled all the way.

"Good going!" Mr. Chapin grinned.

Then it was Nellie's turn. Right away, she fell off

onto the grassy bank and grazed her cheek on a rock. But still she laughed, because it wasn't the kind of hurt that stuck around long.

"You're a couple of tough little birds, aren't you," said Mr. Chapin.

"Strong and true as an oxen team," said Nettie.

And when they started giggling, they could hardly stop, because it had been so long since they'd laughed. It had been so long since anyone had cared whether they laughed or cried.

Mr. Chapin ran along beside them as they took turns riding for the better part of the afternoon.

"Now you try it without me," he said.

"I think I just might be able," Nettie said.

Mr. Chapin nodded and rubbed the back of his neck. "I think so, too," he said.

Nettie climbed onto the bicycle. Mr. Chapin held her there, one hand on the handlebars and one behind the seat. Then he gave her a push.

"Pedal, now! Pedal hard!"

"Pedal, pedal! Steer!" Nellie was hopping up and down at the bottom of the ramp, clapping her hands.

Nettie pedaled. She sat up tall and still and held the handlebars straight and pedaled hard. "I'm doing it!" she hollered. The air whooshed past her ears and blew back the hair that had come undone from her braids. Some kind of insect hit her cheek, and she didn't even flinch. She was riding a bicycle all by herself. She was flying!

So *this* was what a forever home felt like. *Wheeee!*

CHAPTER 13

The promised day came at last. School!

"Class, say hello to our new friends, twin sisters Nellie and Nettie Chapin." Miss Archibald, the teacher, stood with them at the front of the classroom. It was strange to hear their last name announced as Chapin and not Crook, and Nettie felt a jolt of surprise as she looked out over the classroom full of students. There, in the back, was that boy they'd seen at the grocery store, the boy they *knew* was Joe Wilson. He drew his newsboy cap down low over his face and ducked his head.

"Hats off, Will Coffin," Miss Archibald called to him. "You're new here, too, and we don't yet know each other well. But if I see that cap on your head again, you and I will get to know each other better after school." Joe pulled the cap from his head and leaned forward to stuff it in his back pocket.

Miss Archibald had made room for the twins in seats up front that were side by side. But sitting right behind them was Abigail Beebe. She yanked Nellie's nicely brushed hair hard enough that her head snapped back. "Chapin's your last name now, Pig? They only got you off the train, just like a crate of canned corn from California." Nellie ducked her head and reached up where it hurt.

Nettie scowled. Reverend Beebe had preached that they were supposed to leave all their wrath and vengeance-taking up to God. But it was hard not to want to grab up every one of Abigail Beebe's pencils and snap them in half right in front of her face. God might not mind a little thing like that, but Miss Archibald probably would.

It was a long morning, relieved only by read-aloud time. Miss Archibald read to the class from a brand-new book called *The Secret Garden*. In it, they met an orphan named Mary Lennox.

Schoolchildren busy at work in the classroom in 1900.
[LC-DIG-ppmsc-04830]

"Dirty orphan, just like you," Abigail hissed. "Nobody wants dirty orphans."

Why did Abigail have to be so mean? Some folks just were. She was surely cut from the same bolt of awful cloth as Gertie Chapin. Nettie reached for Nellie's hand and squeezed, *one-two-three.*

"'One of the new things people began to find out in the last century was that thoughts,'" Miss Archibald read aloud from the book, "'just mere thoughts—are as powerful as electric batteries—as good for one as sun-light is, or as bad for one as poison.'" She looked up hopefully at her students. "Think of it!" she said.

Nettie thought *poison* was a good word for Abigail Beebe.

Miss Archibald looked again to the open book in her hands and read on. "'Surprising things can happen to anyone who, when a disagreeable or discouraged thought comes into his mind, just has the sense to remember in time and push it out by putting in an agreeable, determinedly courageous one. Two things cannot be in one place,'" she read.

Miss Archibald pushed her eyeglasses up the bridge of her nose with one finger, then raised that finger to make a point. "'Where you tend a rose, my lad, a thistle cannot grow.'" Her eyeglasses slipped again, and she looked over the rims at Nellie and Nettie, and smiled with what Nettie took to be understanding and encouragement. But if Miss Archibald really understood and wanted to encourage them, she should have kept old Abigail Beebe after school.

At lunchtime, some of the children walked home to eat, and others, like Nellie and Nettie, stayed at school and ate from their lunch pails. A shadow fell across

Nettie's legs, which were stuck out in front of her on the grassy bank beside the school. She looked up and shielded her eyes with her hand and studied the boy up and down, from his orphanage-issue boots to his newsboy cap.

The boy pushed the cap back on his head. "Can I sit here?" he said.

"Sure you can," said Nettie, "but tell us, who are you going to be today? Will Coffin? Joe Wilson? Jimmy-John Doo-Hickey?" She took a bite of her sandwich.

"We knew it was you in the store, Joe," added Nellie.

Joe dropped his lunch pail on the grass beside the girls and sat down. "Shoot," he said. "Aunt Jane"—he glanced at the girls—"that's what I'm supposed to call her," he explained, "she and her mister are mortal ashamed they don't have their own boy or girl. I don't know why. But they don't want anybody knowing they got me off the train, see."

"No, we don't see," said Nellie.

Joe looked at her and cocked an eyebrow. "Don't tell me nobody's made fun of you, Nellie Crook. 'Dirty orphan'? 'What's wrong with you if your own parents didn't want you?' Stuff like that?"

Nettie had heard all those things. But she thought of what Miss Archibald had read from that story, the part about pushing out discouraged thoughts and putting in agreeable, courageous ones in their place.

"You see your brother yet?" Nettie asked instead.

Joe's face instantly clouded, and he shook his head. He picked up a blade of grass and threw it. "Nope," he said. He sniffed and dragged his sleeve under his nose.

Nellie patted his shoulder. "He said he'd find you," she said. "Maybe he will."

"Even if he did, Mr. and Mrs. Coffin would turn him away," he said. "Supposably, I'm their nephew, forevermore, and my parents are dead." He picked another blade of grass and tugged it between his fingers. "That part's true, anyhow," he said. "Our parents died a long time ago."

Nettie took a bite of the apple in her lunch pail and chewed, thinking. "Remember what Miss Archibald read out loud," she said after a moment, "about tending a rose so the prickly thistle won't grow?"

Joe and Nellie nodded.

"I wonder," Nettie went on. "You think those apples we chucked out the train windows are gonna grow into apple trees?"

Joe sniffed again. Then he nodded. "I can picture 'em," he said, "all dressed in pretty pink blossoms." He glanced at the girls and flushed red.

"I can picture 'em, too, Joe," said Nellie.

Nettie leaned back on her elbows in the grass. She remembered the bad dream she'd had that night on the train, the dream where she was falling from high up and deep inside an apple tree. *Nobody will know you were here . . . nobody will know you. . . .* She took a deep breath and made herself have a courageous thought. "I can almost smell 'em."

That evening, Mr. Chapin worked late at the store. The girls helped Mrs. Chapin prepare the supper.

Mrs. Chapin cooked almost every meal from a cookbook titled *How to Make Good Things to Eat.* The book was published by a company called Libby, McNeill & Libby. And every single recipe featured Libby's canned goods, which Mr. Chapin had in plentiful supply at the store, as Nellie and Nettie well knew from helping to stack the cans three high and five deep on the shelves.

Nellie and Nettie had flipped through the

cookbook more than once to pass the time during Mrs. Chapin's naps. There were recipes for Libby's Ham-burger Loaf (served cold), Libby's Chicken and Tongue, Libby's Ham Loaf with Creamed Potatoes, and Libby's Ox Tongue Salad, which included a half-peck of spinach that only made it worse. They'd cooked recipes with Libby's chipped dried beef. They'd opened cans of Libby's Vienna sausages, and Libby's hog and hominy. If Nettie didn't know any better, she'd have thought all food came in cans.

But tonight's meal was fish. Pale white haddock fried in butter in a pan, with lots of little bones to pick out. Even *How to Make Good Things to Eat*'s recipe for something called Fricadillen was better than Mrs. Chapin's full-of-bones white fish, and Fricadillen was made out of stale breadcrumbs.

"Clean your plate," said Mrs. Chapin. She used her fork to point at Nellie's dish, set before her on the table.

Nellie's plate was clean. She had eaten all of the canned carrots, and all of the canned corn, and all of the pan-fried fish. All that was left was a small pile of bones and a bit of rubbery gray skin.

"She ate everything you gave her," Nettie said. "All that's left is the bones."

Mrs. Chapin stared at Nettie. Her eyes were as cold as that fish they'd had to eat. The only sound was the click of her knife as she set it on the rim of her plate. She wiped her mouth with her napkin before speaking again.

"I said, finish every last bit of your good supper," said Mrs. Chapin. "Bones and all."

"Why, you old—"

Nellie stopped Nettie with a tiny shake of her head.

Nettie swallowed back her anger and kept quiet. It was hard to watch Nellie choke down those fish bones. They must have gone down like thistles in her throat. This couldn't have been what Miss Hill had in mind when she placed them out. Surely, here, no rose could ever grow.

CHAPTER 14

Winter came, and with it, snow—dry snow, in drifts pushed by strong winds across the land. Was it only a year ago that they'd played in the snow at the orphanage? If only Pops Wendell would appear out of the falling flakes, wearing his coat with the furry collar and wiggling his furry mustache, to help them build a snowman. If only he would come and tell them how all would be well, one day.

Christmas was a sorry holiday. Even in their poorest times, even when Mama was gone for long stretches and Father was away dredging the Erie Canal, they'd managed to celebrate Christmas with a special meal and usually a gift. Christmas here meant a long church service spent pretending that Abigail and Henry were nice friends, and extra work preparing a big meal out of *How to Make Good Things to Eat*, all to Mrs. Chapin's cruelly exacting standards. At night, they pretended their painted spoon dolls were their real family, and they hugged each other under the blankets and softly sang to lift their spirits.

"Silent night, holy night
All is calm, all is bright."

———————

Winter passed, and then it was spring again.

It was just past lunch one Saturday when the sky went green. Nellie said her ears felt like they were stuffed with cotton, and then her eardrums popped. Nettie's head ached. Then they heard the roaring.

"Run!" hollered Mrs. Chapin. Her bulldog cheeks trembled. "Tornado!"

Nettie raced out the door behind Mrs. Chapin, pulling Nellie behind her.

A tornado in Oklahoma City, sometime between 1913 and 1917. *[LC-DIG-hec-02269]*

Nettie thought she heard Nellie calling out. She looked over her shoulder. Nellie was hollering, "Wait!" Nettie shook her head, still moving forward against the wind, following Mrs. Chapin. Her skirts whipped against her legs. It was so hard to move. "Wait!" came Nellie's cry again, like a kitten mewling. "Dolly!"

Nettie shook her head and tugged on Nellie's hand. "Come on!" she yelled.

The wind was whipping so hard it seemed like it was chasing them in particular, as if the sky wanted to swallow them up. They ran to a wooden door set in a frame on a low earthen ramp. Mrs. Chapin yanked the wooden plank back on its hinges to reveal a dark hole in the ground and pushed the girls down inside it. Nettie stumbled.

"Dolly flew out of my hand!" Nellie said. "I had her with me, and then she was gone." She started to cry. Nettie found her in the dark and held on tight.

In the next instant, Mrs. Chapin was beside them in the hole, and the door slammed shut behind her. The tornado roared as loud as the orphan train going full blast, and they were sealed down inside the storm cellar, underground.

Nettie shivered in the dark, tight place with the wooden cover. It was like being inside baby Sissy's coffin, with the candles lit at each end. A flint struck, and then came the spit of a flame. Mrs. Chapin's face was lit suddenly by a lantern. She looked all waxy in the strange light. "We'll wait it out here."

"What about Mr. Chapin?" said Nettie.

"He'll have gone down cellar at the store," she said.

Nettie clung to Nellie and forced herself to keep still. Never had anything like this happened back East. They had huddled together through the dramatic thunderstorms that lit up the sky now and then, especially in the hot, humid summers, but there was a kind of thrill in a thunderstorm, and Mama or Father or at least Leon had always been there with them. This was different. The whole world rumbled overhead, sounds of things dragging and cracking and bumping, like giants having a terrible fight that would shatter the earth.

Nettie squeezed Nellie's hand. Then she began to speak to Nellie in a quiet way, to comfort her, and to comfort herself, the only way they knew how. "Once upon a time," she said, "there were two little princesses—"

Mrs. Chapin abruptly thrust the lamp at them, and they put up their hands and blinked against the light. "This is no time for fairy tales," she hissed.

Long minutes passed, and the world went quiet again. Mrs. Chapin pushed up against the storm cellar door, and they all crawled out and peered around, blinking in the light. Nettie looked up. The sky was as clear and blue as could be, as if the tornado had never happened.

But the tornado had left its mark. The yard was littered with branches. The entire strip of ornamental trim was gone from the porch, and so were the front porch steps. Some shingles had been torn away from the front slope of the roof.

Mrs. Chapin surveyed the damage. "Seen worse," she said. "More of a nuisance than anything, this time."

"Dolly's gone," said Nellie.

Mrs. Chapin looked at Nellie with flat eyes. "My dog blew away when I was a girl, ripped right out from my arms," she said. "And I didn't cry. Mother said to buck up." She looked skyward. Her mouth worked, like she was chewing on something. "And that's what I did," she said after a minute. "Buck up."

Mrs. Chapin bent to pick up a lone shingle from the ground. "I put Scotty right out of my mind, is what," she said, and walked on toward another torn shingle.

Nettie touched the back of Nellie's hand. "You can have Min sometimes," she said.

CHAPTER 15

School let out, and the summer passed in a humid haze. Long hours of work in the garden were brightened by the occasional day spent at the grocery store or fishing with Mr. Chapin, and the seasons changed again.

One day in that long year of 1912 was worse than all the others. The girls were helping prepare the nightly meal. Min sat on the kitchen windowsill, smiling her red-painted smile. Nellie was humming softly, putting the hot supper dishes on the table, when she tripped on a corner of the rag rug. Down she went. The special divided serving dish crashed to the floor and broke, scattering green beans and boiled potatoes everywhere.

"Idiot girl!" screeched Mrs. Chapin. She grabbed the spoon doll from the windowsill and hit Nellie across the shoulders with it, once, twice, three times. Enraged, her bulldog face red and shining, she threw the doll on the floor and yanked the buggy whip from the hook beside the door, raised her arm high, and brought the short lash down. Nellie cried out and put up her hands, but Mrs. Chapin gripped her upper arm and pulled her to standing. Again, the whip came down, again and again.

Nettie threw herself on Nellie's attacker, but Mrs. Chapin swatted her aside and knocked her flat on the floor. Nettie got up and pummeled Mrs. Chapin's back with both fists.

Again, Mrs. Chapin flung her off. Then she turned and clapped the side of Nettie's head and pushed her hard. Nettie banged her head on the edge of the table when she went down. Her ears rang, and she felt blood trickle down the side of her face. Nettie got up on hands and knees but could go no further. "Please!" she moaned—a desperate cry, a prayer. "Please, God, make her stop!"

But Mrs. Chapin did not stop. She whipped Nellie across the back and shoulders and legs till her clothes tore and her skin showed through the slashed woolens on her legs.

Then Mrs. Chapin seemed to realize what she was doing. She stopped. The buggy whip hung limp in her hand, and she turned away.

<hr/>

When Mr. Chapin came home from the store, his wife was sitting at the kitchen table alone, eating her supper. Potatoes, beans, and the pieces of the broken dish still littered the floor.

"Gertie?" Mr. Chapin said. He removed his hat and twisted it in his hands.

Mrs. Chapin kept chewing and did not speak.

"Gertie, where are the girls?"

Mrs. Chapin swallowed and picked her teeth before turning to her husband and gesturing with her fork at the mess on the floor. "You see what they done," she said.

Later, after he'd put ointment on Nellie's cuts and helped Nettie bandage them, Mr. Chapin brought some food upstairs to the girls' room.

"Here's some soup and bread," he said, "plus a bottle of cold Coca-Cola." He set a tray of rattling dishes on the table under the window. Then he fished around his pockets. "And here I brung nice new hair ribbons from the store, one for each of you, so you can tie 'em up matching, the way you like." He reached into his pocket again. "And a pack of chewing gum." His hands shook as he passed a slim packet of Wrigley's Spearmint to Nellie. She took the pack and smiled weakly.

"You don't want to chew that around Mrs. Chapin," he said. He rubbed a hand down over his face, and for a moment, his small chin quivered. "She doesn't like chewing gum," he added in a trembling voice.

Nettie looked numbly at the pack of gum. Mrs. Chapin didn't like a lot of things.

Mr. Chapin closed the door quietly behind him,

and Nettie heard his footsteps clump heavily down the stairs. They ate their very late supper, glad they didn't have to go downstairs and see Mrs. Chapin after what she'd done. Then they changed into their nightgowns.

Nellie lay down on her tummy, so as to cause less pain to her wounds. She put her head on the pillow and closed her eyes. "Tell a story, will you, Nettie?" she said in a small, tired voice.

Nettie sat on the edge of the bed, looking straight ahead at the wall, and cleared her throat. "Once—" she started, stopped, and tried again. She didn't know if she could trust her voice. "Once upon a time," she went on, "there were two little twin princesses, as fair as fairies, as gentle as lambs, and as strong and true as an oxen team." She paused for Nellie to make the sounds of the lambs and the oxen.

But Nellie was quiet.

Nettie swallowed hard and looked down at her hands in her lap. She didn't know if she could keep going with the make-believe. "The twin princesses loved each other," she said, her voice breaking.

"Go on," said Nellie after Nettie was quiet for too long.

Nettie sniffled, and Nellie lifted her head from the pillow. "What is it?"

"I wish I could have stopped her, Nellie," Nettie said, "but I couldn't." She dragged the sleeve of her nightgown across her nose.

Nellie rested her head on the pillow again. "There isn't anything you coulda done, and there's nothing we can do. We're stuck here in this awful place."

Would this really be their forever home?

———◦◦◦———

It would not be the last time Gertie Chapin took out the buggy whip. But one small, good thing came on the heels of the whipping. When Nellie showed up in class with cuts and bruises, Abigail's taunts abruptly stopped. "I fell off a bicycle," Nellie told the children. Maybe Abigail, of all people, didn't believe Nellie's lie.

CHAPTER 16

One winter morning, Nettie went out in the cold to visit the privy. On her way back to the house, she stopped in her tracks. She hugged her arms against the chill and squinted. Her toes were cold in her boots, and she stomped her feet. Coming up the road was a smart buggy pulled by a pair of chestnut horses. As she stood and watched, the passenger's hand reached up, raised in greeting. By instinct, Nettie lifted her hand. When the buggy drew closer, she imagined she knew the woman sitting beside the driver. *Mama?* Her heart beat fast, in time with the horses' clip-clopping.

The passenger began to hop down from the buggy

without even waiting for the driver to come to a complete stop in front of the house. And across the frozen ground stepped someone she and Nellie had thought they'd never see again.

Of course it was not Mama. It was Miss Anna Laura Hill, the Children's Aid Society caregiver who had been so kind to them on the orphan train. There she was in her dark wool cape and matching hat. There was her broad smile, her twinkling eyes, steely now with determination, the lines of her forehead creased with concern.

"Nellie?" Miss Hill peered doubtfully at Nettie.

Nettie shook her head. "It's Nettie," she said. "Oh, Miss Hill!" She ran into Miss Hill's open arms. "It's awful, here. Please, please don't make us stay. This can't be our forever home, it just can't."

Miss Hill embraced Nettie firmly and stroked her hair. Then she held her at arm's length. "Let's go inside, shall we?"

Nettie gazed with longing at the horses stamping their feet impatiently and blowing clouds of steam from their nostrils. "Do we have to?" she said.

Miss Hill smiled. "I suppose not," she said. She

snapped open that big handbag of hers and reached inside. "Here," she said, passing to Nettie the end of a knitted scarf as she tugged the length of it out of the bag. Nettie recognized it as Miss Hill's knitting project on the train. "You go and wait in the buggy with Mr. Picket," said Miss Hill. At the mention of his name, the driver nodded pleasantly and tipped his cap. "There's a blanket on the seat."

"And Nellie?"

"I'll send her out directly." Miss Hill snapped shut her handbag, strode up the porch step, and rapped on the door. *One-two-three.*

CHAPTER 17

And so it was that Miss Hill took Nellie and Nettie away from that house that very day. They had lived there for sixteen long and terrible months. But it was not to be their forever home after all. Someone had reported Gertie Chapin's cruel treatment of the girls, and word had made its way to the Children's Aid Society. From the moment she learned that the girls had been placed out to an unhappy home, Miss Hill wasted no time. The girls wondered who it was who had told on Gertie Chapin and sent the message to New York City. Was it Abigail? Was it Mr. Chapin?

Mr. Picket drove the buggy back to McPherson, Kansas. Nellie and Nettie sat on the backseat of the buggy, their spoon doll, Min, between them. He drove the buggy past the opera house, and Nettie remembered the day sixteen months before, when they'd left here with the Chapins. It seemed so long ago. Now they would live with a new family. But Miss Hill had placed them out with horrible Gertie Chapin. How did she know the new family would not be the same?

"It's only temporary," said Miss Hill. "You will stay with Mary and James Darrah for now, just till we find you a permanent home."

Late in the afternoon, the driver stopped the horses in front of a big, beautiful house on a quiet street.

They were met at the front door by a gray-haired woman wearing a calico dress and a crooked smile. "Come in, come right on in," Mary Darrah said. Her voice was fast and loud. But not angry-loud, not preachy-loud. It was friendly-loud, like she had quite a lot of friendly feeling to get off her chest, and she couldn't do it fast enough. She ushered them into a large front room decorated with painted pictures of sky and hills and trees. The big front windows were hung with pretty blue drapes. And on the floor was a floral-patterned carpet.

An old yellow dog got up from the rug at the same time that a man rose from a stuffed chair. The dog sniffed their hands, and the man greeted them with a gentle handshake each.

"I'll have to figure a way to tell you two apart," Mrs. Darrah said, peering first at one, then the other. "This is my husband, Mr. Darrah, and while you're here you just call me Aunt Mary. Everybody does. This is Spot," she said, reaching to scratch the dog's ears. Nettie glanced at Nellie and grinned. That dog didn't have one single spot on him.

"Now, we'll leave your things in the parlor, here," said Aunt Mary, "and go through to the dining room straightaway. I've got supper ready. Nobody goes hungry in this house, I can tell you."

To all of Aunt Mary's comments, Mr. Darrah added a nod or a smile or a "that's right." No demands were made upon the twins to speak or to explain or to sing "Jesus Loves Me."

Miss Hill went on her way with promises to write, even though Aunt Mary invited her to stay for a meal.

And what a meal! There was a roast chicken Aunt Mary had kept warming in the oven, and hot buttermilk biscuits ("These'll only take a jiffy"), tomato and rice soup ("I make this whenever someone's feeling poorly"), a baked hubbard squash ("Would you like some butter and brown sugar on that, dears?"), and salmon loaf ("You have to try the little bit I give you, but you don't have to finish it, because salmon loaf is Spot's favorite thing in all the world. Of course, I've picked out all those pesky bones"). And for dessert? Lime sherbet ("Mmmmmmm").

That night they went to bed early, stuffed full of Aunt Mary's delicious food. Mr. Darrah brought their things upstairs to their new bedroom.

"I figure you want to share a room," Aunt Mary said, "but if you don't want to, you could each have a room of your own. We've got five bedrooms, after all. Plenty of room. This is the one our Jim slept in when he was a boy. It gets the nice light."

Mr. Darrah and Aunt Mary stood in the doorway and said good night. They were not like Mama and Father. These people were old, more like grandparents. Nettie wondered about their own grandparents. What had they been like?

"Bedtime is kept to the minute," Aunt Mary was saying. "Mr. Darrah and I raised our Jim on early bedtimes, and he's raising our five grandchildren on early bedtimes, and while you're with us, you'll have an early bedtime, too."

Mr. Darrah put his arm around his wife's shoulders and gave her a peck on the cheek. "Dear, I believe these two tuckered-out children would be fast asleep and dreaming by now if you'd quit talking and leave 'em be." It was the most he'd said all evening.

Aunt Mary chuckled and waved with the hankie she had tucked in the cuff of her sweater sleeve. "Sweet dreams," she said, and then the door gently closed.

The next day, after a hearty breakfast ("Spanish eggs, Mr. Darrah's favorite"), Aunt Mary took Nellie and Nettie into town to buy them some new clothes ("I don't know how long you'll be staying with us, but I won't have you shivering while you're under my roof"). A tall, skinny, long-necked woman was coming into the clothing store as they were on the way out, and Aunt Mary introduced the girls to her.

"Well, don't you know, Mrs. Jones, we're keeping them up at the house with us, till they find a new family," Aunt Mary said in her big, friendly voice. "We've plenty of room."

Mrs. Jones looked the girls up and down and then leaned close to Aunt Mary's ear, as if they were friends sharing secrets. "I'm glad you're not taking them in for good," she muttered, loud enough for Nellie and Nettie to hear. "Who knows what runs in their blood? There's no knowing *how* they'll come out."

Mary Darrah nodded. "Mmm-hmm," she murmured, and, "Yes, that's so," she agreed.

Nettie chewed the side of her thumbnail, where a little bit of skin never healed right. It was true. They did not know what awful things ran in their blood. They never knew what had happened to break their family apart, and why that old battle-ax Matron at the orphanage thought it better to send them on the orphan train than to give them to the aunt who had come for them. Nettie frowned and stared at the lady.

"But then again, dear," Mary Darrah said sweetly to Mrs. Jones, tipping her gray head to one shoulder, "who knows how your *own* children will come out?"

Nettie snorted and hid her grin behind her hand. The woman drew her chin into her neck like a startled goose, clutching her handbag to her chest, while her mouth gaped open and shut. After a moment, she closed her lips primly. If Mrs. Jones was anything like that old Abigail Beebe, she'd have ready another barb, just as sharp.

But instead, the woman started to laugh. "Oh, Aunt Mary, how right you are," she howled. She tipped her head back on her goose-neck and laughed good and hard. Aunt Mary shrugged, and laughed along with Mrs. Jones.

Then Mrs. Jones turned to the girls. "You like peanut butter cookies?"

Nettie nodded. "Yes, ma'am."

"We sure do," said Nellie.

"My cookie jar is always full," said Mrs. Jones. "How 'bout you come over and have some. Tomorrow work for you, Mary?"

Aunt Mary nodded, apparently struck dumb.

"Very good," said Mrs. Jones. And she went past them into the store.

"Well, blow me over with a feather," said Mary Darrah. "Will wonders never cease?"

CHAPTER 18

Late one afternoon in early March, the sky grew wild and dark. Clouds gathered on the horizon, and the air grew thick. Little whorls of dirt and grit skittered along the road, kicked up by the wind. Nettie and Nellie were setting the table for supper, and Aunt Mary was stirring good-smelling stew in a pot on the stove.

"Looks like some weather's moving in," said Aunt Mary. She tasted the stew, nodded once, rapped the wood spoon on the pot rim, and set it on the counter. "Just right," she said. "I'm a good cook, if I say so myself," she said, turning from the stove. It was true that Nellie and Nettie did not miss one single recipe from *How to Make Good Things to Eat.* "What is it, my dears?" Aunt Mary said when she saw Nellie's and Nettie's faces.

Nellie set a fork on a folded napkin and glanced nervously out the window. "Is it a tornado?"

"No, dear," said Aunt Mary, "it's just a good old storm. Nothing to worry yourselves over, though Spot doesn't much like thunder." She leaned slightly and patted her thighs so that Spot would come to her. She rubbed all along the dog's back, and he closed his eyes and whined with pleasure.

"It isn't tornado season, you see," she said, "and if it was, why, we'd just hustle out to the storm cellar and get cozy. Spot, too." She crossed the room, leaned over the kitchen table, and looked out the window, then pulled out the chair nearest the window and sat.

"Come here," she said to the girls. She put her arms out to draw them to her. "You want to know what I like to do sometimes, when there's a good storm coming through? The kind like this, with big dark clouds rolling in, maybe some rumbly thunder?" She looked eagerly out the window, peering at the sky as she spoke. "Unless I'm tucked into the storm cellar, I like to sit safe right here at my kitchen table and watch that storm come in. And then I watch it roll on out again. And I say to myself, 'Well, Mary Darrah, isn't that just the way of it?'"

Aunt Mary turned from the window. She tilted her head and gave a sad smile that seemed to take in all of the girls' past, and maybe their future—a smile that seemed to mean *I understand*. Nettie smiled back. It felt good to have someone smile at her that way.

"Storms rage in the life of every person." Aunt Mary spoke in a quiet voice, almost a whisper. "As long as I draw breath and walk the earth, the storm may come, and come again, and that's the God's truth. But it's just as true that every storm will pass, given time." She nodded knowingly. "It will." She put a gentle hand on each girl's shoulder. "Do you take my meaning?" she asked.

Nettie thought of the storm clouds in their lives: losing Mama, and Father, and their baby sister. She thought of Leon. She thought of their friends Brenda O'Hare and Bucky, and the little baby left in a basket at the orphanage, the pretend sister they called Sissy, and she wondered where the winds had tossed them. She remembered that awful, dark night in the storm cellar, when they were huddled together, trembling, and how Mrs. Chapin told them it was no time for fairy tales. She wondered, back then, if the storm would ever break.

But it did. That storm moved on. And they were here, now, in this bright kitchen.

Nettie chewed the inside of her cheek. "You want to know what *we* like to do when a storm comes through?" she said.

"Yes, dear," Aunt Mary said firmly. "I most certainly do."

Nettie looked at Nellie. "We like to tell stories."

Aunt Mary smiled wide. "Why, I can't think of any better way to handle a storm," she said. Spot came and rested his muzzle on her knee. "Do tell a story right now, won't you? That stew can wait."

CHAPTER 19

The weeks passed quickly, and it was more than two months later that Miss Hill returned to McPherson and to the big house with two old folks, two little girls, one yellow dog, and five bedrooms.

"Good news!" Miss Hill declared. She fairly burst through the door when Aunt Mary opened it.

"Well, let's hear it, then," said Aunt Mary, ushering Miss Hill inside. She took Miss Hill's dark woolen cape and hung it slowly on the coat tree, as if it weighed a ton. Then she led Miss Hill to the parlor. Spot stayed close on her heels.

"I've found you girls a new home—a forever home, isn't that how you put it?" Miss Hill said, sitting back with a triumphant smile. "You'll be happy there, I know it. It's up in South Dakota, on a farm," she said, splaying her fingers as if she was scattering magic fairy dust. "It's lovely—pretty as that picture on the wall," she said, pointing to one of Aunt Mary's paintings. "The family comes highly recommended and is most eager to have two special girls like you."

Nettie watched Miss Hill's mouth move as her voice went on talking about the big farmhouse, and the nice mother and father, and the barn cat's new kittens, and the weather there in spring.

Forever home. Family. It was everything she'd waited for.

Nettie grabbed her sister's hand in both of hers and squeezed. Nellie's eyes told Nettie she felt the same. Finally, they would have what they'd always wanted.

And they didn't want to go.

CHAPTER 20

"**C**ome and get it!" shouted Aunt Mary, though these days Nellie and Nettie called her Mother Darrah. It was September, and it was Sunday morning, the day of the twins' baptism. After the morning service, there was a big lunch on the grass outside the Congregational church.

"Come and get your fried chicken. Come and get your green salad and your macaroni salad. I've got sheet cake and shortcake and apple pie, too." Mother Darrah's delicious food was spread out on a folding table, and not one single thing had come out of a Libby's can. It seemed like half of McPherson had turned out to welcome Nellie and Nettie, now known as the Darrah twins, into the church family.

———◦◦◦◦———

Six months had passed since Anna Laura Hill came to call at the big house and take the girls away to their forever home in South Dakota.

Nellie had knelt and buried her face in the ruff of Spot's neck, and the good old dog had howled along with her sudden tears.

Nettie had opened her mouth to speak but found she couldn't say the words. What if they didn't have any choice about South Dakota? What if they *had* to go? Worse, much worse—what if Aunt Mary didn't want them to stay? Hot tears sprang to her eyes, and she wiped them away. She started again to explain, but Aunt Mary spoke for her.

"We've grown very fond of Nellie and Nettie here," she said, addressing Miss Hill. "Isn't that right, James?" She went on without even waiting for Mr. Darrah's reply, which was a hearty nod and a "Yes, that's so, dear." "And the thing of it is, we'd—well . . ." She jammed her fists into her hips. "We'd like for them to stay with us. Here." She pointed at the parlor's floral-patterned rug. "For keeps."

Nettie squeezed her eyes shut to stop the tears from falling. She could hardly believe her ears. Could it be true? Did Aunt Mary and Mr. Darrah want them—really *want* them? Forever?

Aunt Mary clasped her hands under her chin. "Can't we keep 'em as our own?" she said. "Can't our dear girls stay?"

Silence filled the room. Everything was as quiet as Aunt Mary's paintings of sky and hills and trees. They held their breath and waited for what Miss Hill would say next.

And what she'd said was "Yes."

"I've brought my famous peanut butter cookies," sang Mrs. Jones now, on the green grass outside the church. "I know you Darrah twins love 'em." Mrs. Jones winked at Nellie and Nettie, and they grinned back. For someone who had wondered what bad blood might run in the veins of two placed-out girls, Mrs. Jones sure made good cookies, and her cookie jar was always full, just as she'd promised them the day they met.

The minister, Mr. Fellows, wandered over to the girls, carrying a plate of chicken and macaroni. "My apologies, again, Nellie," he said, looking straight at Nettie, "and Nettie," he said, turning to Nellie, "for mixing the two of you up, and baptizing you in the wrong names." He gazed up at the vast blue sky. "But the good Lord won't mind, if you don't," he said.

Nettie grinned. They never minded being mixed up. That was half the fun of being identical twins, with matching braids and matching ribbons in their hair. The other half was always having a best friend, right there handy. No matter what, no matter where.

Mother Darrah cut a slice of apple pie and put it on a paper plate. "Here you go, Nettie," she said. Nettie reached for the plate but Mother Darrah didn't let go, so for a moment, they were holding it between them. "I've always said we have plenty of room in the house," Mother Darrah said. "But I hope that you know— surely you girls must know by now—we also have plenty of room in our hearts." She nodded once and let

go of the plate. "Now go and eat your apple pie, and here's a piece for Nellie. There's more if you want it."

Nettie went over and sat beside Nellie on the grass. The pie tasted wonderful—buttery, sweet, and tart, with lots of cinnamon.

"You ever think about those old wormy apples we threw from the train?" Nettie said.

Nellie nodded and managed, "Mmm-hmm," her mouth full of pie.

"You figure the train conductor was right, and people will know we were there?"

"Mmm-hmm." Nellie's mouth was still full.

Nettie slowly finished her pie. She didn't believe anybody would ever know that two twin girls had planted some of those apple seeds along the route of the orphan train. But it didn't matter. Because somebody in particular knew Nettie and Nellie now, really *knew* them. Somebody loved them.

Nettie reached for Nellie's hand and squeezed, *one-two-three*. Then she went and got them each another piece of apple pie.

Nettie and Nellie Crook as fifth-graders in 1916.

AUTHOR'S NOTE

I don't know if it's better to remember or forget the hard
things that happened to us in our lives. Mother Darrah made
up for much of the bad, and we both had long, happy marriages.
Miss Hill made certain that Nellie and I were kept together,
and that was the best thing. Without my twin, everything
would have been much different for me.

—NETTIE CROOK DARRAH ENNS, INTERVIEWED IN *WE RODE*
THE ORPHAN TRAINS, BY ANDREA WARREN

Before homeless shelters, before today's foster care
system, before adoption agencies, the Orphan Trains
chugged west, bearing children from the streets of
Eastern cities to homes with families in every state.
During the second half of the nineteenth century in
America, there were essentially two methods of deal-
ing with the poor: preaching at them or imprisoning
them. In 1853, a young minister named Charles Loring

Brace introduced another way. He founded the Children's Aid Society to serve destitute children— tens of thousands of them—in New York City. Central to his goal of providing children with meaningful work, education, and functional families was a placing-out system (as distinguished from placing-in programs such as orphan asylums) that became known as the Orphan Trains. All told, approximately 250,000 children were Orphan Train riders, including twin sisters Nettie and Nellie Crook.

The term *orphan train* was not in use at the time Nettie and Nellie rode west accompanied by Anna Laura Hill. *Orphan train* is used here because the term has become widely recognized today. Less than half of the riders were actually orphans, though, and many, like Nettie and Nellie, had two living parents.

Not all of the Orphan Train riders' stories were happy ones, and there were critics of the system. Most of the riders were white, like the families they were placed with, who were largely of Western European descent and wanted children who would be most like themselves. Children older than fourteen were typically not placed out. Sickly or disabled children, too,

High-school-age Nettie and Nellie Crook
photographed in 1920.

Babies at the Children's Aid Society. *[LC-DIG-ggbain-01464]*

were not likely to find homes. And while many children became full members of loving families, many were taken in only to provide hard labor, many were housed in barns or attics, and many were abused. Nettie and Nellie were fortunate to have been removed from the Chapins' house. They never knew who reported their abuse at the hands of Gertie Chapin, but they were forever grateful.

In the story, Nettie is curious about the number of children at the orphanage, and Joe is surprised to learn that there are other children riding the orphan trains.

Why were there so many poor and homeless children? New York City saw a flood of people after the opening of the Erie Canal in 1825, which made New York the gateway to trade with the East Coast and the Midwest. After that, and across the turn of the century, approximately a thousand people a day poured into New York

The Children's Aid Society at mealtime.
[LC-DIG-ggbain-01462]

City from overseas and from all parts of the United States. Around the same time, New York saw riots, rising crime, and a widening income gap between rich and poor. Cholera epidemics, typhoid and tuberculosis, alcoholism, society moving into the Industrial Age while maintaining in many ways the attitudes and expectations of a farming and small-town era gone by—this is some of what set the stage for the problem of homeless children destined for lives of misery.

But not so for Nettie and Nellie Crook. Once settled with Mary Darrah and her husband (who died a short time later), the girls led happy, ordinary lives. They were excellent students who eventually worked

Nettie and Nellie Crook photographed with their husbands. Both women married in 1930 and celebrated fiftieth wedding anniversaries.

their way through Kansas State University. When both married in 1930, Miss Hill sent each young woman a wedding gift. With marriage came a parting and separate lives, but late in life they lived right across the street from each other. As adults, they did reunite with their older brother, Leon, and with their father, who cried over them but never explained what caused the family to split apart. Nellie was the first-born twin, and she was the first to pass away, shortly before the twins turned 92. Nettie passed away in 2003, at age 98.

> *It is important—even consummately important— not to obscure the connection between the orphan trains and our own child welfare programs, because the consequences of [Charles Loring] Brace's moral effort end—if they may be said to have ended at all—only now, in this moment, and in each succeeding moment, as we ourselves decide what we can and should do to help the "poor and friendless" children of our own time.*

—STEPHEN O'CONNOR, *ORPHAN TRAINS: THE STORY OF CHARLES LORING BRACE AND THE CHILDREN HE SAVED AND FAILED*